THE
HIDEOUT

Books by Peg Kehret

Available from Simon & Schuster

THE
HIDEOUT

PEG KEHRET

Simon & Schuster Books for Young Readers

New York   London   Toronto   Sydney   Singapore

SIMON & SCHUSTER BOOKS FOR YOUNG READERS
An imprint of Simon & Schuster Children's Publishing Division
1230 Avenue of the Americas, New York, New York 10020

Copyright © 2001 by Peg Kehret
First Minstrel Books hardcover printing April 2001
First Simon & Schuster Books For Young Readers printing July 2002

SIMON & SCHUSTER BOOKS FOR YOUNG READERS
is a trademark of Simon & Schuster.

Printed in the United States of America
10 9 8 7 6 5 4 3 2

ISBN: 0-671-03420-0

For Kevin Konen,
who would be the perfect son-in-law
if he didn't eat all the apple crisp

CHAPTER

1

It was all so senseless. That was the worst part; Jeremy's parents were gone for no reason.

If they had died of a terrible disease or even been killed in a car wreck, Jeremy might have been able to accept it. But Mr. and Mrs. Holland did not even know the man who had run into the mall waving a gun and shouting curses at the government.

Jeremy's parents had just finished their shift as volunteers in a Humane Society exhibit that urged people to spay or neuter their companion animals. As they walked toward the mall exit, the crazed man rushed in.

They were the first people he saw, and the first

1

of six whom he shot before two brave bystanders overpowered him and wrenched the gun from his hands. Mr. and Mrs. Holland simply happened to be in the wrong place at the wrong time.

Fate. That was what Jeremy's best buddy, Paul, had said. "It was fate."

Jeremy couldn't buy that. If someone had spotted the gunman sooner and called the mall security guards, and the man had been taken away without shooting anyone, what then? Would Jeremy's parents have choked on their dinner or been hit by a truck in the parking lot because fate said they were supposed to die at a certain time?

No, Jeremy thought. It wasn't fate; it was bad luck. It was plain bad luck that a madman with a handgun had entered the mall just as Jeremy's parents were leaving it.

Jeremy and Paul had been at a movie. Paul's dad had picked them up and driven Jeremy home.

"Hey, look!" Paul had said as they started down Jeremy's street. "There's a police car in front of your house."

Paul's dad pulled up behind the police car and got out with Jeremy. Paul followed.

Two officers approached. "Jeremy Holland?" one of them asked.

"That's me," Jeremy said.

"I have bad news for you. I'm sorry."

2

Paul's dad had driven Jeremy, white-faced and shaking, to his grandmother's apartment.

The next few days passed in a blur. Jeremy stayed with Grandma and helped plan a memorial service. He read condolence cards and answered the phone and accepted deliveries of flowers.

He watched television news accounts of the shooting and saw an interview with his dad's friend, Kyle, a fellow volunteer in the Humane Society exhibit that night.

Jeremy picked at food brought in by friends: lasagna, potato salad, chocolate cake. Nothing tasted good. Even the big container of snickerdoodle cookies that Paul's mother brought, knowing they were Jeremy's favorites, did not tempt him. He simply had no appetite.

Uncle Ed arrived from Chicago to help with the arrangements. He was the brother of Jeremy's mother, but they were as unlike as two siblings could be.

Jeremy's parents had lived a simple life. They had steady jobs and an attractive small home in Seattle, but personal fulfillment was more important to them than income. Because they believed it was important to preserve the earth's resources, they hung clothes outside to dry to save electricity. They composted all vegetable scraps, digging the compost back into their garden. They commuted to work on the city bus and worked only thirty hours a week in order to have time for volunteer activities.

Through the county parks department they planted hundreds of seedlings to stabilize the banks of salmon streams. They raised funds for libraries and helped animal welfare groups.

By contrast, Uncle Ed was marketing director for a national appliance company. He worked sixty hours a week, lived in a fancy house, drove luxury cars, and thought his sister and brother-in-law were quaint. For relaxation, Uncle Ed usually went skiing in Switzerland or took a Caribbean cruise.

There was never a family feud, but over the years the contact between Jeremy's mom and her brother had dwindled to a letter at holiday time, supplemented by reports from Grandma.

That was why it had come as such a shock to Jeremy when, the day after the memorial service, Grandma told him, "You'll be going to Chicago next week to live with Ed."

"I don't want to live in Chicago," Jeremy protested. "I want to stay here."

"I'm sorry, Jeremy. I would keep you here if I could but you know that isn't possible."

"I could help you, Grandma. I can learn to cook, and I don't mind sleeping on the sofa. We could tell the visiting nurse not to come every day."

Grandma's eyes filled with tears, as they had so often in the last few days. "If I were healthy," she said, "I would move to a two-bedroom apartment and you and I would do just fine together. But you can't replace the nurse, Jeremy. I need help bathing, and before long I may need full-time care. That isn't a job for you, no matter how much you love me."

Jeremy knew she was right. "Why can't I stay in my own house? I've stayed by myself before."

"Not overnight."

"No," Jeremy admitted, "but I've stayed alone lots of times. I haven't had a sitter for over a year."

"Thirteen is not old enough to live alone," Grandma said. "Ed listed the house with a real estate agent this morning."

Jeremy felt as if he had been punched in the stomach. "He's going to sell my house?"

"The proceeds will be held in trust for you, along with the funds from your parents' life insurance. Ed is merely handling the business on your behalf."

"I don't want to sell the house. He has no right to do that!"

Grandma put a finger to her lips, shushing Jeremy. "Your parents had a will," she continued. "It named Ed as your legal guardian."

"Then why isn't he telling me all this?"

"He felt it might be easier for you to hear it from me. He's trying to do what he thinks is best for you."

Grandma took a handkerchief from her sleeve and wiped her eyes. "I know Ed and your parents did not agree on many issues," she said, "but Ed is a kind and honest man. Your mom and dad believed that too, or they would not have asked him to be your guardian."

"When did they choose him?" Jeremy wondered.

"Not long after you were born. They wanted to be sure that if anything happened to them, you would be provided for."

Jeremy was stunned. His parents had known for thirteen years that Uncle Ed was Jeremy's guardian, yet they had never told him.

"Why didn't anyone tell me before now?" Jeremy asked.

"I suppose they didn't want you to worry about something that wasn't likely to happen."

"But it did happen."

Jeremy's stomach churned. The worst thing that could possibly happen to him was now a reality.

CHAPTER
2

The next afternoon Jeremy and Paul went to Jeremy's house to pack his clothes and other belongings. He had decided not to take any furniture.

Uncle Ed drove them. "You're sure you don't want me to help?" he asked, as they carried empty boxes into the house.

"No, thanks," Jeremy said.

"I know how hard this is for you," Uncle Ed said. "After Maria died, it was two years before I could open her closet."

Jeremy said, "Maria?"

"My wife. We had been married less than two years when she died of cancer."

"How long ago was that?" Jeremy asked.

"Eleven years. I still miss her every day."

"I'm sorry," Jeremy said. "I don't remember her."

"She loved you," Uncle Ed said. "She was thrilled when your parents asked us to be your guardians."

Jeremy was silent, absorbing this new information.

"You never got married again?" Paul asked.

"No. I put all my energy and time into my work." He put a hand on Jeremy's shoulder. "Pack whatever you want to keep. I—that is, we have a big house."

"Thanks," Jeremy said.

"Call when you're ready to leave," Uncle Ed said.

When the boys were alone, Paul said, "He doesn't seem so bad."

"He's trying," Jeremy admitted. "Grandma says at my age I need a male role model."

"You already have a male role model," Paul said. "You have me."

Despite his grief and his frustration at having to leave his home, Jeremy laughed. "Maybe that's why I'm being sent away," he said. "Because I hang out with a nutcase who is a bad influence on me."

The boys grinned at each other, but their smiles quickly faded.

"I'm going to miss you something fierce," Jeremy said.

"There's always e-mail," Paul said. "I'll write every day."

Jeremy clung to that small comfort. Paul would not be there to shoot baskets with him and listen to music and complain about too much homework, but at least Paul would send him e-mails every day. It was better than nothing.

"You'll make new friends," Uncle Ed said that night when Jeremy mentioned that he and Paul planned to write daily.

"I don't want new friends," Jeremy said. "I want Paul. He's been my best friend since first grade."

Grandma interrupted. "Paul will always be your friend, Jeremy. Just because you make new friends doesn't mean you have to give up the ones you already have."

Uncle Ed tried to paint an optimistic picture of Jeremy's future in Chicago. "I'll find a top-notch private school for you," he said, "and you can take lessons in tennis and golf this summer. When I have to be away, my housekeeper, Mrs. Moyer, will be there. She's an excellent cook."

Uncle Ed gave Jeremy a picture of his house, a three-story white Victorian with formal landscaping. "Your room overlooks the garden," he said, pointing.

Jeremy stared at the photograph. He and his parents had grown tomatoes and green beans and sweet corn in their small backyard garden. Uncle Ed's garden had topiary trees, pruned into unnatural shapes, and a bronze sculpture.

How could he live in such a place? It looked like a hotel.

"Hey," his friend Alison had said, when Jeremy showed her the picture, "living with a rich uncle sounds cool to me. You'll probably get your own phone and TV, and when you're sixteen he'll buy you a red convertible. Ask him if I can come, too."

Jeremy had laughed at Alison, but he did not change his mind. He seriously considered running away, but he had nowhere to go. Grandma and Uncle Ed were his only relatives, and he would be found instantly if he stayed with one of his friends.

Uncle Ed planned to fly back to Chicago on Sunday. Jeremy wanted to go to school on Monday, to give his new address to his friends and to say good-bye. Uncle Ed suggested that Jeremy take the train on Tuesday.

"The train ride will let you see what this great country looks like," Uncle Ed said. "It's hard to believe you're thirteen years old and have never been out of the state you were born in."

To Jeremy, the words sounded like an accusation that his parents, by never taking him on a cross-country trip, had somehow failed him.

"I've seen the ocean," Jeremy said, "and the mountains, and the desert in eastern Washington. We camped someplace different every summer."

"There's a whole big world outside of Washington State," Uncle Ed said. "You haven't lived until you've seen New Orleans and Paris, but a train ride to Chicago is a start."

"The train is okay with me," Jeremy said. He was in no hurry to get to Chicago, and a train ride from Seattle might be soothing, give him time to sort out his feelings.

Three days later he was on the train, but instead of calming him, the journey made him more agitated. Every turn of the wheels took him farther away from his school, from his friends, from the only home he had ever known.

Jeremy felt as if his whole world had fallen apart, as if he were in one of the pictures they show on television after a terrible hurricane. The world had collapsed, and he was left standing alone in the rubble.

The train sped on. Rain poured down, streaking the windows.

The dark skies matched Jeremy's mood. He wished he could hop off at the next stop and live alone somewhere. Anywhere. It wouldn't be as good as being at home with Mom and Dad, but it would be better than where he was going. On his own, at least he could be himself instead of trying to fit into Uncle Ed's life-style.

The engineer blew the whistle whenever the train went through a town or crossed a road. To Jeremy, the whistle's long mournful howl was a good-bye to the life he loved.

Fighting back tears, Jeremy put his backpack against the window, leaned his head on it, and closed his eyes.

A deafening noise woke him.

The train whistle was blowing short, sharp, urgent blasts. At the same time Jeremy heard the shrill screech of metal scraping on metal.

Pressing his face to the window, he saw only wilderness in the dusk outside. He glanced at his watch. He had slept nearly two hours.

The whistle kept blowing. The screech grew louder.

Apprehension crawled up Jeremy's arms as he realized the screech was coming from the train wheels scraping along the tracks as the train worked to stop quickly.

Other passengers cried out, "What's happening?" "What's wrong?" "Hang on!" Their words jumbled together in a medley of anxiety.

Jeremy clutched the seat with both hands and braced his feet against the floor.

Crash!

The noise of the impact filled Jeremy's ears, momentarily blocking out all other sounds.

Jeremy fell sideways out of his seat, landing in the aisle. His backpack came down on top of him.

The lights inside the train went out.

The din of disaster surrounded him: glass shattered, wood splintered, pieces of metal clanged against one another.

The whistle was silent.

Inside the dark car, people screamed. A baby cried.

Crash!

The second crash came from the rear, and Jeremy realized the car behind his had smashed into the one he was in. His head jerked forward, clunking painfully against the metal of the seat beside him.

As he struggled to keep from being flung into the air, he felt the car rise off the tracks like an airplane lifting off from the runway.

The bitter taste of fear filled Jeremy's mouth.

CHAPTER
3

Still on the floor, Jeremy felt the train shift sideways. For a moment he feared it was going to flip over.

The wheels on the left side of the car hit the ground first. This jolt threw Jeremy into the air.

The car teetered for an instant, then smashed against the ground, landing on its side.

As it skidded down an embankment, it bumped upward and crashed down again several times, hitting rocks and crushing small trees.

Inside, Jeremy hit the floor, bounced up, and landed on the floor again. Seats tore free and slid into a heap, trapping people beneath them. Jeremy curled up into a ball and held his backpack over his head with both arms.

Purses, shoes, and lunch coolers tumbled on the terrified passengers.

Something hard slammed into Jeremy's back. He cried out, but kept his head down.

Windows broke, sending shards of glass flying through the darkness.

When the car finally shuddered to a halt, the screams and shouts of the passengers continued.

Jeremy raised his head, surprised that he was alive. Cold water dripped on his head even though he was still inside the train. Someone shone a flashlight overhead and Jeremy saw that an emergency exit had popped open on the side of the train that now faced upward. It was only about six feet ahead of him.

A voice behind him said, "We can climb out there, through that exit!"

A man trying to push forward stomped on Jeremy's leg.

Jeremy still clutched the strap of his backpack. He slipped the pack on his back, then crawled over a pile of debris until he was directly under the exit door.

Standing on a toppled seat, he grasped the side of the doorway and hoisted himself up through the opening. He stood on top of the side of the train, some twenty feet off the ground. Wind whipped the rain against him.

Other people also climbed up through the door. Their voices ran together in a chorus of unanswered questions: "What happened?" "Did we hit another train?" "Can you see a way to climb down from here?"

Moans and cries for help came from those still inside the car.

As the train cars on the tracks above him continued to crash forward, Jeremy saw another car break free. A few passengers who had gathered on a small observation platform at the back of the car jumped off.

The wheels on the far side of the car rose up off the ground. The car twisted sideways and lurched down the embankment toward the car that Jeremy stood on.

"It's coming this way!" the man beside Jeremy shouted. "It's going to crush us!"

There was no time to climb down. As the huge car skidded toward him, Jeremy leaped off the train, away from the approaching car.

He landed in gravel, slid a few feet on his side, then rolled to his right.

Everywhere, people shouted, screamed, begged for help. Jeremy looked up just as the engine exploded. Flames leaped into the air, lighting the horrible, destructive scene.

Jeremy saw what had caused the wreck—a huge

mud slide. The pile of mud and rocks, as big as a house, had slid downhill like an avalanche and covered the train tracks. The engineer, coming around a curve, had only enough time to blow the whistle and apply the emergency brakes before the train plowed headlong into the heap of mud and rocks.

Jeremy counted nine railway cars off the tracks. One was upside down; one was upright but condensed to half its original size, with its ends pushed toward its center. The rest of the cars, including the one he had been on, all lay on their sides.

Lightning crackled overhead, followed by a loud boom of thunder. Rain continued to assault him, running down the back of his neck and snaking inside his shirt collar. Jeremy thought about taking his jacket out of the backpack, but decided against it. He was soaked to the skin already. It was too late for the jacket to help.

Blood trickled down Jeremy's cheek, where his face had hit the gravel. He wiped it off, aware that his new shirt was ripped and dirty. I'm lucky to be alive, he thought.

He heard a low moan not far away and went to investigate. An elderly man lay on the ground, his legs pinned under a piece of steel that had broken loose from the train. A lump the size of half a tennis ball had risen on the man's wrinkled forehead.

"I'm here," Jeremy said.

The man's eyes flickered open. He seemed to be Grandma's age or older. "I was—thrown out," the man gasped. "My legs . . ."

"I'll try to free your legs."

"Thank you."

Jeremy grasped the piece of steel and tried to raise it off the man's legs. He lifted until his muscles twitched from straining so hard, but the steel was too heavy for him. Next he knelt beside the man, put his shoulder against the steel, and tried to push it off.

Sweat ran down Jeremy's face, the salt stinging his cuts and scratches. Still the steel didn't budge.

Out of breath from the effort, he rested a moment beside the man. "I'll find someone to help," he said.

"No," the man whispered. "Don't leave me."

Jeremy hesitated.

The man spoke haltingly, resting between words. "I feel better with you here," he said. "If you go for help, I'll be alone."

"Were you traveling with someone?" Jeremy asked.

"By myself."

Jeremy turned toward the burning train and shouted, "I need help over here!"

His call blended with dozens of other cries, and went unanswered.

When nobody came, Jeremy stayed beside the old man. He removed his jacket from the backpack and held it over the man's head so the rain wouldn't hit him in the face.

"Talk to me," the man said. Jeremy could barely make out the words.

"It's a terrible wreck," Jeremy said. "We hit a mud slide. The engine and two of the cars are burning. I can see people running and some lying on the ground, but a lot of passengers must still be inside."

Then, realizing that hearing about the train wreck was no solace to the man, Jeremy said, "I'm on my way to Chicago, to live with my uncle."

The man groaned.

Panic filled Jeremy. He didn't want this man to die. He had lived with too much death already.

"I think I should get someone to help you," Jeremy said.

"No. Please." The words were like spiderwebs, thin and fragile, with spaces between them. "Talk—more."

Jeremy couldn't think what to say. Finally he

told how he had used a potato peeler last summer to scrape his name on a pumpkin when it was green. "As the pumpkin grew in our garden," Jeremy said, "so did my name: Jeremy. I had a personalized jack-o'-lantern for Halloween.

"My parents always did fun things for Halloween. One year they put chunks of dry ice in a bucket of water and set it by our front door. When kids came to our house for trick or treat, they walked through cold steam that was bubbling out of the bucket."

A smile flickered over the old man's lips. His hand moved slowly across his chest and reached inside his suit jacket.

"Another year," Jeremy said, "Dad filled an old cotton garden glove with mud, and had it sticking out the end of his sleeve. After kids took their candy, Dad stuck out the glove, as if to shake hands. Of course, when the kids took hold of the glove it felt all squishy and they all shrieked and laughed."

Jeremy had begun talking as a way to console the old man, but as he put his memories into words, he realized he was comforting himself as well. His parents were gone and his life was forever changed, but no one could take away his remembrances of happy times.

The old man slid his hand out of his pocket and

held a money clip full of currency toward Jeremy. "For you," he said. "For your kindness."

"I can't take your money," Jeremy protested.

"My—family—has plenty." The man coughed again, a shuddering sound that filled his entire body. He pressed the money into Jeremy's hand.

Just then a young man came toward them, carrying an injured woman.

"Can you help me?" Jeremy called. "This man is trapped under a piece of steel and I can't get it off him."

The young man laid the woman on the ground, then hurried to the old man's side. As the young man bent toward the piece of steel, Jeremy shoved the money into his jeans, let his jacket rest on the old man's face, and grabbed the piece of steel with both hands.

"One, two, three, *lift!*" the man said. Both of them struggled, but the steel stayed where it was.

"I'll come back with help," the young man said, "but first I need to try to get people out of the train. Dozens are still inside, and the fire is spreading."

The man ran off.

Two helicopters buzzed overhead, sending searchlights across the train. The lights swept over the hillside, and Jeremy knew the helicopter pilots were looking for a place to land.

Jeremy bent over the elderly man, lifting the jacket again but keeping it over the man's face for protection.

"Help is on the way," he said. "Helicopters are landing; someone will be here soon."

There was no answer, but the old man nodded slightly.

"Other people are trapped in the burning train," Jeremy continued. "I'm going to try to help them get out."

The man nodded again.

"I'll come back to you as soon as I can," Jeremy said.

Jeremy gently replaced his jacket over the man's face, then ran toward the closest railway car.

Before he reached it, another explosion blasted from the center of the flames. Blazing debris shot into the air like a fireworks display. The earth shuddered as a horrible smell filled the air.

"My baby!" screamed a woman. "I have to get my baby!" Two people held her back from rushing into the fire. It was too late to rescue anyone from such an inferno.

Jeremy stumbled on, toward the train.

"Don't look back," Grandma had told him when she hugged him and said good-bye. "The past is over, and the only way you can get to the other side of this terrible time is to go forward."

Now, it seemed, he had gone forward into an even worse situation.

CHAPTER

4

Smoke thickened the air. The fire spread to more cars.

The rain eased, and the thunder now rumbled far in the distance.

Jeremy joined a clump of people who watched helplessly as flames consumed five railway cars. Intense heat made it impossible to approach the train.

"There'll be hundreds dead," one man predicted.

"We may never know for sure how many," another said. "With heat like this, they won't be able to identify the bodies."

"The railroad line has a passenger list," said the

young man who had tried to help Jeremy lift the piece of steel. "If your name is on the list and you don't get rescued, they'll know you didn't make it out. Your family will get a call from a railroad representative or from the police."

Jeremy did not want to think about all the families who would be notified, the way he had been notified, that their loved ones had died.

The young man saw Jeremy and said, "Is your friend still trapped?"

Jeremy nodded yes.

"I'll need help," the young man said, and two men went with him toward where the old man lay pinned under the piece of steel.

Jeremy followed the men. He couldn't bear to watch the wreck any longer. He didn't want to hear any more cries. After the steel was lifted, he would stay with the elderly man and try to block out the man's pain with happy memories.

As he walked into the darkness, he tripped on a picnic basket that had been thrown from the train. Jeremy stumbled, then fell, hitting his head on a rock.

He sat up, feeling dizzy. He wondered where he was and why his clothes were so wet.

He got to his feet. When he saw the blazing train, he remembered the wreck. He looked toward the old man; people were helping him.

Numb with shock, Jeremy walked away from the disaster, not knowing or caring where he went. He walked past the flames, past the crumpled railway cars, past hysterical people and injured people.

Jeremy kept going, stumbling through low bushes and climbing over rocks. When the last car was behind him, he climbed up the embankment and walked along the railroad tracks. His eyes soon adjusted to the darkness and he found it easier to follow the tracks than to walk through the brush.

The rain stopped, but by then Jeremy was too wet to care. He trudged on, wanting to put as much distance as possible between himself and the train crash.

In his dazed condition, he gave no thought to where he was going or to what he would do when he got there. He wanted only to escape—to flee from tragedy and horror over which he had no control.

Jeremy walked until his weary legs could go no farther. Then he headed down the embankment away from the tracks, lay on the damp ground beneath a tree, and fell asleep.

Some time in the night, half awake and half asleep, Jeremy remembered who he was and where he had been going on the train.

He opened his eyes, wide awake now and filled

with excitement. He recalled what the men had said the night before about the victims: it would not be possible to identify everyone.

Jeremy knew his name would be on the passenger list; if he was not found, he would be presumed dead.

This is my chance to escape, he thought. I can walk away and start a new life, and nobody will know where I am.

He felt a twinge of guilt when he thought of inflicting more grief on Grandma, but it was outweighed by the prospect of making a life for himself away from Chicago, away from Uncle Ed's pretentious life-style.

He would keep walking and change his name and find a way to live that did not involve a stuffy prep school in Chicago. Smiling to himself, Jeremy went back to sleep.

Sunlight woke him. He blinked and sat up as memories of the night before returned. His legs and back ached, and hunger gnawed at his stomach.

He took a sandwich from his backpack. Uncle Ed had laughed at Grandma when she said she would pack food for Jeremy.

"Plenty of food is available on the train," Uncle Ed had said.

"Junk food, no doubt," Grandma had replied, "at exorbitant prices."

Uncle Ed had admitted that meals on the train were expensive.

Grandma had packed sandwiches, baby carrots, two apples, and a bag of her homemade ginger cookies. Now Jeremy was grateful for every crumb.

I should go back, Jeremy thought as he ate. I should turn around and walk to the train wreck. I should let the railroad people know that I'm alive. I should call Uncle Ed and have him arrange for me to get to Chicago.

He closed his eyes and lifted his face to the warm sun. He did not want to turn back. He did not want to call Uncle Ed. Not yet. He knew that his middle-of-the-night fantasy of never returning, of changing his name and starting a new life, was not practical. Where would he live? How would he support himself?

That idea had been born of his dreams, and in the clear light of day, with the shock of the train wreck wearing off, Jeremy knew it could never happen.

But that didn't mean he had to return right away. Maybe he could have a short time by himself and then go back.

Just a day or two of independence, Jeremy thought. Just a little time on my own and then I'll call Uncle Ed and tell him where I am. I'll claim I had amnesia and didn't remember my name. I'll say I was in shock, which is probably true, and I wandered away from the wreck and didn't know who I was, which wasn't true, but it might have been.

He checked the contents of the backpack carefully: a shirt and underpants, toothbrush and toothpaste, two more sandwiches, plenty of cookies, one apple, an unopened bottle of spring water, three books, and his wallet, which contained the forty dollars that Uncle Ed had given him in case he needed anything while he was traveling.

He had enough food and water to last two days, if he ate sparingly. Perhaps he would come to a town where he could buy more food. He could get a loaf of bread and a jar of peanut butter and some juice. Maybe a few bananas or some grapes. He could eat for quite a while on forty dollars. He could last on his own for more than a couple of days.

A week, Jeremy thought. One week to be all alone, and then I'll go back. One week didn't seem like too much to ask, given what Jeremy had been through.

The prospect of an entire week of total independence glowed in Jeremy's mind like a secret treasure. For the first time since the night Paul's dad drove him home from the movie and Jeremy saw the police car waiting for him, he had something to look forward to.

He wrapped the second half of the sandwich he was eating and saved it for later.

He returned to the railroad tracks and continued walking in the direction he had been going the night before—away from the crash.

He walked slowly, savoring his freedom. It was amazing to think that nobody in the entire world knew where he was.

He heard only the crunch of his shoes on the gravel between the railroad ties. I need this, Jeremy thought. I need time alone.

Ever since the shooting, he had been with other people—good, kind people who tried to comfort and help him—but now Jeremy felt an overwhelming desire for solitude.

As the sun rose higher, Jeremy got too warm. When he saw what appeared to be an animal path leading away from the tracks into a grove of trees, he followed it. He knew deer often walked the same route day after day, creating a path. He tried to move quietly so that if he came upon any deer he would not startle them.

The shade cooled him. The smell of pine and cedar surrounded him while the pungent scent of decomposing leaves rose from underfoot.

He continued deeper into the woods, knowing

he would not get lost because he could turn around and follow the animal path back to the tracks.

He found a fallen tree a short distance from the path and decided it was the perfect place to sit while he ate the other half of his sandwich. He had planned to wait until late afternoon to eat again, but walking gave him an appetite. He was ravenous, in fact. After having no interest in food for over a week, he could hardly think of anything else. He sat on the tree and opened his backpack.

As he ate his sandwich, a twig snapped not far behind him. He heard another twig, then another. Something was moving toward him.

Jeremy looked, expecting a doe or a buck. If he sat still enough, perhaps the deer would walk past him on the path. He had never seen a deer up close before.

As he watched, a black bear ambled into view, following the trail toward Jeremy. It had its head down, snuffling along the ground, and had not yet seen Jeremy.

Jeremy's stomach knotted up.

Was the bear following Jeremy's scent? Did it know how close he was?

Why had he assumed it was a deer approaching?

CHAPTER

5

The bear swayed from side to side as it walked. Jeremy realized it was because the bear lifted both right feet at the same time, and then both left feet.

Everything Mom and Dad had ever told him on camping trips rushed to his mind. He was to do one thing if he saw a grizzly and something else if he saw a black bear. To his dismay, Jeremy could not remember which was which. Should he run? Climb a tree? Should he stand and wave his arms and shout at the bear, or should he sit still and then, when the bear saw him, stare at it until the bear backed away? What if it didn't back away?

While he sat paralyzed with indecision, two

cubs came down the path, trailing after the bear. Jeremy saw the cubs at the same instant that the bear saw Jeremy. Her head jerked up. She looked at him for a moment. The cubs stopped moving toward him.

Jeremy knew that any wild animal would defend its young. A mother bear with cubs was the most dangerous bear of all.

The bear dropped her head and turned sideways. Does that mean she feels threatened? Jeremy wondered. Or is she just going to graze?

He waited.

The bear looked at him again. She watched Jeremy for a long moment; then she stamped her front feet on the ground. She growled and made a blowing noise. She swatted the earth with her paws.

It seemed clear to Jeremy that the bear was warning him to get away from her and her cubs.

The cubs climbed six feet up a cedar tree, one on either side of the trunk. They clung to the bark, watching their mother.

Jeremy stood up slowly, hoping the bear would not charge him. He needed to get back to the path. If he had to turn and run, he could go much faster on the path than if he tried to run through the tangled undergrowth.

He couldn't go directly toward the path; that

would take him too close to the bear. Instead, he moved sideways, easing away from her, trying to rejoin the path as far from the bear as possible.

When Jeremy moved, the bear stopped swatting the ground, but her ears went flat against her head. She growled again. The hair on her spine stood on end, the way a cat's fur did when it was frightened.

She means business, Jeremy thought. She wants me out of here. He tried to move faster but vines tangled around his shoes and clung to his legs, and thick brush blocked his way so that he had to zigzag toward the path.

The bear growled louder.

Jeremy finally reached the path about thirty feet in front of the bear. He wished he could go back the way he had come, toward the railroad tracks, but the bear stood between him and the tracks. She continued to growl and slap her paws on the ground.

Jeremy walked backward, going deeper into the woods. Before each step, he felt the ground with his feet, hoping he would not trip and fall. It was easier walking now that he was back on the path, but there were still places where roots and rocks studded the ground, and large ferns, salal, and huckleberry bushes hung over the path, catching his clothing.

The bear watched him move away from her. Then she stiffened and began to hop toward Jeremy, her legs as straight as fence posts. She growled with each hop.

Jeremy was still holding the rest of his sandwich. Maybe that's what the bear wants, he thought. Maybe she smells the bread and cheese.

Hoping to distract her, he tossed the uneaten sandwich toward the bear. It landed a few feet in front of her. One of the cubs leaned sideways to look and fell out of the tree.

The mother bear quit hopping, went to the sandwich, and swallowed it in one gulp.

That was too easy for her, Jeremy realized. I need to make her spend some time getting the food—enough time for me to get away.

He hated to part with any more of his food. Without it, he knew he would have to walk back to the train wreck and identify himself. He couldn't live on his own if he had nothing to eat.

Given a choice of returning and calling Uncle Ed or getting mauled by a black bear, Jeremy definitely chose life in Chicago.

He slipped the straps of his backpack off his shoulders and flung the entire pack toward the bear. It landed with a thud on the path between him and the bear. He kept walking backward as he watched the bear approach the backpack. The cub that had fallen out of the tree followed her; the other cub still clung to the tree trunk.

The mother bear briefly sniffed Jeremy's backpack. Then she swiped one paw across it, ripping it open as easily as if she had pulled a zipper.

Jeremy shuddered, thinking what those claws could do to him. He watched the bear as he kept backing away from her.

The bear stuck her muzzle inside the backpack, clearly smelling the rest of his food.

Jeremy heard the crunch-crunch as she ate the remaining apple.

The path curved then, and Jeremy backed out of sight of the bear. He decided that this was the moment to run. The bear was busy with Jeremy's sandwiches and ginger cookies, and she could no longer see him.

Jeremy turned and ran as fast as he could. As he raced deeper into the forest, he focused his attention on the path behind him, listening for the sound of growling or branches breaking, or other signs that the bear was following him.

He heard nothing but his own footsteps and his own gasping breath.

He ran until a crick in his side forced him to stop. Still listening for the bear, he sat on a stump to catch his breath. The woods behind him were quiet except for a chittering squirrel. If the bear had chosen to chase him, Jeremy felt sure she would have caught him by now.

I got away, he thought. This time. But what do I do now? The bear ate all my food—and how many other bears are there in these woods?

He couldn't go back the way he had come, for fear of meeting the mother bear and her cubs again. But without any way to protect himself, he didn't want to continue deeper into the forest, either.

He thought about avoiding the path and trying to circle back through the woods to the railroad tracks. The underbrush was thick and hard to walk through; it would be easy to get lost if he left the path.

Earlier in the day he had rejoiced in the knowledge that no one knew where he was. He had felt independent and adventuresome.

Now he just felt scared. He could have been killed by the bear or, worse yet, mauled and left alone in the woods. He would never have been found because nobody knew where to look for him.

CHAPTER
6

Jeremy's mouth felt as dry as dust. He wished he had removed the bottle of water before he tossed his backpack to the bear.

He estimated that he had walked two hours the night before, and six hours that day before he left the train tracks and entered the forest. He had walked and run a mile or more since seeing the bear.

If he could somehow get back to the railroad tracks, it would still take him eight hours to walk back to the site of the train wreck. That was a lot of walking with no water.

Instead of trying to circle the bear and go back, Jeremy decided to follow the animal path a while longer. Perhaps the path would lead to a stream. If he didn't find water in an hour, he would turn back and retrace the path to the tracks.

By then the bear would surely have led her cubs away from the backpack. Maybe the bottle of water would still be there.

He walked slowly now, listening carefully. He paused frequently to look behind him and on both sides.

He wished he could tell Mom and Dad about the encounter with the bear. What a story! During all the years that Jeremy had gone camping with his parents, they had never seen a bear, although they always worried about bear attacks. They faithfully locked their food in their car and left nothing at the campsite that would attract a bear.

Now, on his first day alone, Jeremy had seen not just one bear but three! They were beautiful animals, their dark fur glossy and thick, and their brown eyes gleaming. If he hadn't been so afraid, he would have been thrilled to see them. He smiled, remembering the curious cub who had fallen out of the tree.

He wanted to rush to a telephone and call Mom and Dad, to tell them all about it.

The sadness that lurked at the edges of his mind pushed in, bringing tears to his eyes. Never again would he dial that telephone number, the number that had been his for all of his life. It had already been disconnected. Never again could he share what happened to him with his parents.

I'll e-mail Paul, he thought, forcing the grief away. As soon as I get to Chicago, I'll send Paul an e-mail, and for the subject heading I'll put "The Three Bears." Jeremy smiled as he thought of Paul reading his letter.

His nervousness began to fade and his sense of adventure returned. Even though he had to give up his plan of being on his own for a few days, he had one exciting memory.

Half an hour farther down the path, he stepped into a small clearing and saw an old log cabin. The logs had weathered to a light gray, and the roof over the wooden porch sagged. Beside the cabin a wire fence surrounded a six-square-foot area that once must have been a garden.

The two porch steps creaked as Jeremy walked up them. He knocked on the door, waited a few moments, and knocked again.

Was it a hunter's cabin, used only in the fall? Was it a summer retreat that sat empty the rest of the year? Or was it an abandoned homestead, long since deserted by its builder?

When no one answered his knock, Jeremy tried the doorknob. It turned. He pushed the door open and peered into the dim interior.

"Hello?" he said. "Is anyone here?"

A mouse scuttled across the floor and disappeared into a hole in the floor.

Jeremy stepped inside, closing the door behind him. The single room had only two narrow windows, and the tall trees outside blocked much of the light from them. He saw no light fixtures or switches; the cabin apparently had no electricity.

A wool blanket covered a single bed, and some wooden packing crates, stacked three high, formed shelves. A fat red candle stood in the center of a small crudely made wooden table. Two wooden chairs sat beside the table.

Jeremy drew a line in the dust on the table. Cobwebs stretched from corner to corner near the ceiling. Jeremy sneezed.

A flashlight rested on top of the crates. When Jeremy pushed the switch, no light came on. It probably needs new batteries, he thought.

A wall-hung cupboard near the table contained several cans of food: baked beans, corn, tomato soup, clam chowder. He found a can opener, two tin plates, a tin cup, a ladle, a large wooden spoon, a roll of toilet tissue, a box of matches, two forks, and a cast-iron kettle. The kettle's blackened bottom indicated that cooking was done over a wood fire.

A smaller table just inside the door held a shallow pottery bowl, a worn green towel, and what was left of a bar of soap.

Jeremy went back outside and walked slowly around the cabin. He found a three-foot circle of large stones surrounding a patch of blackened ground. The campfire area, Jeremy thought.

He pulled vines from a low mound near the fire circle and saw a pile of firewood, split and ready to use.

Most important of all, he saw a rusted pump. When he pumped the handle up and down, water poured from the spout, splashing onto the smooth stones below. The water was cloudy at first but it soon turned clear.

He got the cup from the cabin and filled it with water. He sipped warily, then gulped quickly, draining the cup. The water tasted cold and fresh. Excitement made his breath come faster.

I can stay here a day or two, he thought. It's a safe place to sleep and there's food and water. I'll rest and heal and have some time alone before I go to Chicago.

He pulled two pieces of wood from the pile; they were damp from the winter rains. He wondered who had chopped the wood and how long ago.

I need kindling, Jeremy thought. He searched the edge of the woods near the cabin, gathering small twigs. He wished he had some newspaper.

As he looked for dry kindling, he saw where the animal path continued on the other side of the clearing. Tomorrow he would explore in that direction.

Returning to the fire circle, he built a small pyramid of twigs. He got the box of matches, lit the twigs, and fed the flickering flames with more twigs until the fire burned strong enough to put one of the logs on. When it caught, he returned to the cabin.

He opened the can of tomato soup, put it in the kettle, pumped water into the soup can, added that to the kettle, and stirred it together. Then he poked the fire with a stick and set the kettle next to the burning log.

He leaned over the kettle, trying not to get smoke in his eyes, as he stirred the soup. The side of the kettle next to the burning log got hot first; the soup on that side stuck to the bottom. Jeremy stirred harder.

Steam rose from the kettle; it smelled delicious. Jeremy kept stirring until the soup began to bubble. Then he realized he had a problem: the kettle was now too hot to touch. How was he going to get it off the fire?

He did not remember seeing any pot holders in the cabin. He should have brought the towel out with him, but he didn't want to go back for it. He knew the soup would burn quickly if he left it on the fire without stirring it.

Jeremy grabbed another piece of wood from the stack, stuck it under the kettle's handle, held both ends of the wood, and lifted.

The kettle wobbled as he carried it away from the fire, but the soup did not spill.

Jeremy set the kettle on the ground and, using the big spoon he had been stirring with, began to eat. No meal had ever tasted better to him. He ate every bit, even the thick, dark chunks that had to be pried from the bottom of the kettle.

When he finished eating, he pumped water into the kettle and used a handful of leaves to scrub it.

After he ate, he realized how tired he was. He had been weary when he boarded the train. Could that have been only twenty-four hours earlier? It seemed like weeks ago.

The anguish of the crash, his concern for the injured old man and the trapped baby, and Jeremy's fear of the bears, plus all the walking that day and the night before, had left him feeling as if he could sleep for a week.

After dousing the fire, he returned to the cabin carrying a handful of sticks. He broke the sticks into two-inch lengths and stuffed them into the hole in the floor where the mouse had gone. He worked until the hole was completely plugged.

He took the wool blanket out to the porch and shook the dust off it. Then he removed his shoes, lay on the bed, pulled the blanket up under his chin, and closed his eyes.

Tired as he was, sleep eluded him. He couldn't quiet his thoughts. Was he making a big mistake by postponing his trip to Uncle Ed's house?

If Uncle Ed and Grandma found out he did not have amnesia, they would be angry with him for letting them believe he had been killed in a train crash when all the while he was hiding out in a cabin in the woods. What if Uncle Ed was so angry that he refused to take Jeremy? Where would he live then?

I'll stay here only a day or two, he thought. Just until the food is gone.

After all he had been through, he decided he was entitled to a couple of days alone in the cabin. Grandma and Uncle Ed would have no reason to suspect that he was able to remember who he was. They would believe what he said.

Eventually he slept, but he jerked awake an hour later, instantly aware that a noise outside the cabin had awakened him.

He listened tensely. A branch snapped, not far beyond the cabin door.

Jeremy rose quietly, walked to the window, and peered out.

45

A huge bull elk stood just beyond the clearing. The rack on his head branched upward as he raised his head and ripped leaves from an alder tree. The elk's rump was lighter colored than the rest of his fur. The small alder branches snapped off in the elk's strong jaws.

Thrilled to see such a magnificent creature in the wild, Jeremy watched until the elk moved on into the woods, out of sight.

Jeremy went back to bed. This time he removed his shirt and jeans before getting under the blanket.

He lay quietly, wondering how many people ever saw three bears and an elk in one day. Smiling, he fell asleep and slept soundly through the night.

The next morning as he stepped into his jeans, he realized there was something in one of the pockets. He stuck his hand in and pulled out the money clip that the old man had pressed into his hand. Jeremy had been so shocked and upset at the time that he had completely forgotten about it.

The silver clip bore three engraved letters: JSW. Those must be the old man's initials, Jeremy thought. He wished he had asked the man's name. He wondered if the man had survived.

He removed a thick wad of bills from the clip,

then began to count them. Most were fifty-dollar bills, two were twenties, and three were hundred-dollar bills. All together he had six hundred and ninety dollars!

If he retrieved his backpack, he would also have the forty dollars from Uncle Ed. That made seven hundred and thirty dollars. A person could hide out in the woods for many months with that much money to spend. All he needed was a place to buy food.

CHAPTER
7

He ate cold baked beans for breakfast, washing them down with well water. It seemed like too much trouble to build a fire and scrub the kettle, so he spooned the beans out of the can, picking out the pieces of pork.

When he had eaten, he searched for a tree limb to use as a walking stick. After he found one, he followed the path back the way he had come, listening carefully and moving quietly. If he saw a bear, he planned to wave the stick in the air and shout.

It took him only forty minutes to reach his backpack, which lay in shreds on one side of the path. The food was all gone, and so was the bottle of water. Jeremy wondered if the bear had eaten the plastic bottle or carried it off in her teeth.

His shirt and underpants were too ripped to wear, but his wallet was unharmed. Jeremy removed the money from the clip, put it in his wallet, then shoved the wallet in his back pocket.

One of his books was tattered from the bear's claws, but the other two were intact. Jeremy carried them back to the cabin. Books would give him something to do at night. He could read by candlelight, like Abraham Lincoln.

He returned to the cabin and put the books and the remains of his backpack inside. Then he went to the rear of the cabin, where he had seen the animal path go off in the other direction. He was curious about where it led.

He planned to move about only during the middle of the day, when he would be least likely to encounter wildlife. Still carrying the walking stick, he started off.

He had hiked about a mile when a sudden sound made him stop. A car! Jeremy was certain he had heard a car drive by in the distance. He walked faster.

A few minutes later he heard another car. He was close to a road!

He began to run, forgetting all about staying quiet.

The path emerged from the woods at one end of a narrow wooden footbridge. The bridge spanned a shallow stream.

On the other side of the bridge a gravel road stretched as far as Jeremy could see, both to his right and to his left. A cloud of dust hung in the air over the road, from the last car that had passed.

Jeremy turned right, following the road. Two more cars came by, one from each direction. Jeremy stood on the shoulder of the road while they passed.

The road curved several times; each time he rounded a curve he looked expectantly ahead, but he saw only more road, winding endlessly along.

When the road began to climb uphill, he turned back. He was tired of walking when he reached the footbridge, but he did not return to the cabin. Instead he followed the road in the other direction, too curious not to explore.

This time, as he rounded the second big bend in the road, he saw a building ahead. Jeremy trotted toward it until he could read the sign: Clem's Country Market. The store was similar to small stores in remote areas where Jeremy and his parents had bought supplies on past camping trips.

"Yes!" Jeremy said as he shook his fist over his head. He had found a place to buy food.

Smaller letters on the sign announced that

Clem's Country Market was open for business from 8:00 A.M. to 6:00 P.M. daily.

Jeremy stepped inside.

The store smelled musty. Three elk heads hung on the wall above the counter, their lifeless eyes staring at an old Coca-Cola sign. Remembering the strong, vital animal he had seen the night before, Jeremy looked away. A live elk in the wild was beautiful; a stuffed head hanging on the wall was ugly.

A large man with a bushy beard sat in the corner behind the counter, his chair tilted back against the wall. He wore a stained flannel shirt and dirty jeans.

"Hi," Jeremy said.

The man nodded his head in acknowledgment.

Jeremy walked along the store's only aisle to a cooler at the back. He removed a quart of milk. He also chose a loaf of bread, a jar of peanut butter, and a can of potato soup. He carried everything to the front and put the items on the counter next to a large cash register.

As he did, he saw a hand-lettered sign taped to the countertop: Bear Claw Necklaces, $5.00 each. There was only one necklace next to the sign—a leather thong with a few blue glass beads knotted in it and, dangling at the center, a large curved bear claw.

Jeremy stared at the claw, remembering the way the mother bear had slashed open his backpack.

The man got out of the chair. "You live in these parts?" he asked.

"For a while," Jeremy said. "My family's rented a cabin for a couple of weeks."

"That so?" the man said. "Whose cabin?"

"I don't know the owner's name," Jeremy said.

The man snorted. Jeremy wasn't sure what that meant.

"Are you Clem?" Jeremy asked.

"Yep."

"I'll probably be in to buy groceries every few days," Jeremy said. Maybe if the man thought Jeremy was a good potential customer, he would be friendlier.

"How'd you get here?"

"Now, you mean? I walked."

Clem's eyes narrowed. He stared at Jeremy as if debating whether or not to believe him.

"Didn't know there were any cabins for rent around here."

Jeremy took the wallet from his pocket and removed one of the twenty-dollar bills that Uncle Ed had given him.

The man rang up Jeremy's purchases, took the money, and counted out change without saying anything else.

As Jeremy slid the bills back in his wallet, Clem leaned closer, staring.

Jeremy saw that, when he opened his wallet, he had exposed a hundred-dollar bill, and it was obvious that he had several other bills as well. Even though Clem had no way to know how large those bills were, Jeremy realized that this man now knew he had a lot of money. He snapped the wallet shut and put it in his pocket.

Clem said nothing as he put the groceries in a paper bag, then pushed the bag toward Jeremy. Jeremy noticed that Clem's fingernails were crusted with grease and dirt.

"Thanks," Jeremy said. As he lifted the bag, he looked at the necklace again, fascinated by the size of the claw.

"If you want the necklace," Clem said, "it's yours for only four-fifty. A real steal."

Jeremy didn't want it; he thought it would be creepy to wear a piece of an animal around his neck as a decoration.

"I don't have any money of my own," he said. "This is my dad's wallet, and he'll get mad if I buy more than what he told me to get."

"That claw is from a black bear, a big one. Tell your dad he could get twenty, thirty dollars for that necklace in Seattle or San Francisco."

"I'll tell him," Jeremy said.

"Not many bears left," Clem said. "A necklace like that will get more valuable as time goes on."

"I saw some bears yesterday," Jeremy said.

"You did? How many?"

"Three. A mother with two cubs."

"Were they around here?"

Jeremy wondered suddenly if Clem hunted bears. Had he cut that claw off the paw himself and made the necklace? Even though Jeremy knew hunting season wasn't until fall, he decided not to tell Clem the location of the mother bear and her cubs. The mother bear had scared him silly, but he didn't want her to be killed by a hunter.

"They were a long way from here," he said.

Jeremy's parents had been against hunting, saying there was nothing sporting about using high-powered weapons to kill animals. They had actively campaigned to make it illegal in Washington State to use bait when hunting bears.

Jeremy's dad had been shown on television saying, "Any coward can shoot a bear whose nose is in a bucket of doughnuts." The comment got so much response that the clip was shown over and over whenever the bear-baiting issue was discussed. It even made the national news one night.

For a couple of days after that, his parents had quit answering the phone, letting their machine record the angry voices that accused them of caring more for animals than for people.

Jeremy wondered what Clem would say if he knew that the man who had said the famous doughnut quote had been Jeremy's dad. On the other hand, Clem didn't look as if he spent much time watching news broadcasts, national or otherwise.

"How far away?" Clem asked. "Where were you when you saw the bears?"

Jeremy wished he had not mentioned the bears.

"It was yesterday when we were driving to the cabin—probably seventy or eighty miles from here."

It amazed Jeremy that he was able to lie so easily. He had never before deliberately lied to anyone, at least not since he was old enough to understand the concept of truth, but now the falsehoods rolled off his tongue as if he had been inventing stories forever. First the rented cabin, then pretending that his dad would be angry if he bought the necklace, and now saying the bears had been far away.

When it comes time to tell Uncle Ed I've had amnesia, he thought, I should be plenty convincing.

Instead of making him glad, that thought made him feel guilty. Mom and Dad had told him to tell the truth always. What would they think of his plan to hide out in the cabin?

They taught me to take responsibility for myself, he thought. They would rather have me being self-sufficient in the woods than lounging around Uncle Ed's pool. Wouldn't they?

He carried the bag of groceries to the door.

As he left Clem's Country Market, he had the feeling that Clem was standing at the window, watching to see which way he went.

CHAPTER

8

The conversation with the store owner had made Jeremy uneasy. There was something about the way Clem had watched him put the money back in his wallet, and the way he had tried too hard to get Jeremy to buy the necklace, that made Jeremy want to stay away from him.

With his dirty hands and clothes, Clem certainly did not look as if he ought to be working in a store that sold food.

Jeremy wondered if Clem knew about the old cabin. Had he guessed that Jeremy might be living there? Whether Clem knew about the cabin or not, Jeremy didn't want him to suspect that Jeremy was by himself.

The next time I need to buy food, Jeremy decided, I'll buy shaving cream, too, and say it's for my dad.

He didn't like to think of wasting money on something he couldn't use, but he didn't want Clem, or anyone else, to suspect that he was living alone.

Even though he didn't care for Clem, he was ecstatic to have a place where he could buy food and other supplies. Having the store within walking distance meant that he could stay in his hideout as long as his money lasted.

He made a peanut butter sandwich and filled the tin cup with milk. He realized he had no way to keep the rest of the milk cold, so he drank three cups of it with the sandwich. Next time he would see if Clem sold milk in half-pints, the way Jeremy bought it at the school cafeteria.

After he ate, he sat at the table, thinking. If the country store sold enough merchandise to stay in business, there must be other people living close by. Was he near a town? Were there other cabins in the area, cabins that people used regularly? There must be, because Clem had asked which cabin Jeremy's family had rented.

He wondered where the gravel road led and where it came from. Was he still in Washington or had the train crossed into Idaho before it crashed?

He wished he could ask Clem what state he was in, but that would be a sure tip-off that Jeremy was not telling the truth about renting a cabin with his parents.

From now on, he would not speak to Clem unless Clem asked a question. He had been foolish to say he had seen three bears. Even if Clem was not a hunter, he might mention the bears to someone else.

It wasn't just a matter of protecting the bears; Jeremy needed to protect himself. He didn't want anyone to know about the cabin.

Now that he had a source of food, Jeremy decided to stay in the cabin longer, maybe all summer. Tomorrow he would walk beyond the store to see what was down the road in that direction. Maybe there was another store. He had enough money to buy what he needed. If he was within walking distance of a small town, he might be able to get by without talking to Clem.

Jeremy knew that even if he had an endless supply of money, he could not stay at the cabin beyond the end of August. He had to go to Chicago in time to start the new school year. Unless he wanted to spend his entire life with no indoor plumbing and no contact with other people, he had to finish school. The only realistic way to do that was to live with Uncle Ed.

Besides, he had shipped all of his clothes and personal belongings, including the scrapbooks and picture albums that his parents had kept, to Uncle Ed's house. He had also sent his dad's watch, the little gold locket that his mom often wore that had a baby picture of Jeremy inside, the crystal hummingbird that hung in the kitchen window, and the wooden clock that Dad had built. None of the keepsakes had much monetary value, but Jeremy knew he would cherish them always. They were all that he had left, except for memories.

So he would go to Chicago at summer's end. He would make new friends and go to the school Uncle Ed chose for him, and he would try to live in a way that would make his parents proud.

But not yet. He wasn't ready yet, and there wasn't any compelling reason for him to spend the summer in Chicago. What would he do for three months—take tennis lessons and write to Paul?

No. Jeremy did not intend to call Uncle Ed until the middle of August, and that was three months away.

Excited by the possibility of the whole summer on his own, Jeremy went outside and examined the garden spot. He spent the rest of the afternoon on his knees, pulling weeds and wild grass.

He wished he had a shovel. He chopped at the dirt with the large spoon, trying to loosen it. Tomorrow he would see if Clem sold seeds.

He decided to hide part of the money. It seemed foolish to walk around with hundreds of dollars in cash in his wallet.

Jeremy quickly realized there was no safe hiding place inside the cabin. He wrapped most of the money in the tattered remains of his backpack to keep it dry. Then he removed some pieces of firewood from the pile, put the wrapped money in the middle of the stack, and piled wood on top of it, making sure that the backpack was hidden from every angle.

He counted pieces of wood, to be sure he could find the money quickly if he needed to: ten logs from the left and four logs from the top.

He ate more soup for dinner, along with another peanut butter sandwich. After he washed out the kettle, he heated fresh water, poured it into the shallow bowl, and used the bar of soap to wash his underwear and socks. He draped them over the back of one of the chairs. With any luck, they would be dry by the time he woke up in the morning.

He got in bed and read until it grew too dark to see. It was only seven-thirty, but he decided not to light the candle. Even though there were no people near enough to see a light in the window, Jeremy wanted to stay as inconspicuous as possible.

Back home he would have protested loudly at going to bed so early. Now he welcomed the sleep, as if making up for all the nights that he had tossed and turned at Grandma's house, the nights when he had lain awake remembering his parents and wishing he had been better about showing his love for them.

Dozens of times he had regretfully relived his last conversation with them, yearning to take back his words and replace them with something else.

Mom and Dad had driven him and Paul to the movie theater on their way to the mall. As Jeremy got out of the car, Mom had said, "If you get home before we do, put some potatoes in the oven to bake."

Jeremy, showing off for Paul, had replied, "I'm tired of good nutrition. Let's send out for pizza."

Paul had laughed, and Jeremy had waved at his parents as they drove away. Then he got in line to buy movie tickets.

That had been it. No "Good-bye" or "I love you" or "Thanks for the ride" or even "See you later." Just a smart-alecky remark about pizza.

Now, as Jeremy watched the darkness fill the

small cabin, he forgave himself. They did know I loved them, he thought. Most of the time they were proud of me. I never got kicked out of school or brought the police to our door or did anything to make them wish I was someone else's kid. I made some good birthday gifts for them and I always served breakfast in bed on Mother's Day.

His eyes closed. Dad would make a joke about it, he thought.

He could almost hear Dad's voice saying, "My son's last words to me were 'Let's send out for pizza.'" Then Dad would laugh that deep laugh that always made everyone else in the room chuckle, too, whether they knew what was funny or not.

Jeremy drifted into sleep.

Bang!

Jeremy's eyes flew open. He sat up, his heart thudding. Had he been dreaming, or had he heard a gunshot?

It wasn't yet totally dark out; he must have slept for only a few minutes.

Bang! Bang!

That *was* a gun, Jeremy thought, as fear prickled the back of his neck. Someone was out there in the woods between the cabin and the road. What were they shooting at?

Hunting season was always in the fall, and this was only May. It was too dark for target practice.

Who was out there—and why?

He got out of bed, then carried one of the chairs to the door. He tilted it back so that it leaned against the door on two legs. There wasn't any way to lock the door, but the chair would at least warn him if someone started to come in.

Trembling, he stayed at the window, watching for motion in the woods.

He heard no more shots. He didn't hear voices, either.

Perhaps the gunshots had been farther away than he thought. Noise carried far in the silent forest. Earlier that day, Jeremy had looked for a woodpecker that he heard pecking at a tree trunk, only to find the bird several trees farther away than he first thought.

Could the sound have carried that well if it had come from the road? Was it possible that he had not heard a gun at all but merely a car backfiring?

No, he told himself. He had heard gunfire. He was sure of it.

Someone had fired a gun when it was almost dark. What if a person—what if Jeremy—had been walking in the woods? The gunman would never have seen him.

Dusk slid into darkness. Stars popped into view over the trees.

After waiting for more than an hour, Jeremy decided that whoever had been out there was gone. He got back into bed and lay staring into the dark, listening to a tree branch rub rhythmically against the edge of the roof.

CHAPTER
9

When he awoke the next morning, the chair was still leaning solidly against the door. Jeremy went outside and walked slowly around the edge of the clearing. He saw elk tracks but no human footprints except his own. There were no empty shotgun shells or cigarette butts or any other sign that someone had been there the night before.

He was sure the shots had come from deep in the woods, toward the road, and it was a relief to see that whoever had fired them apparently had not come near the cabin.

As he ate bread and peanut butter for breakfast, he thought about Mom's homemade cinnamon rolls and Dad's special Saturday pancakes, served with real maple syrup. I never knew how lucky I was, he thought.

After he ate, he walked out to the road and headed east toward Clem's Country Market.

Three cars went by, all driving from west to east. Jeremy had figured out directions by watching the sun rise and set. He still didn't know what state he was in, but at least he knew that the cabin faced north, the animal path he had followed went north and south, and the gravel road ran east and west.

Just before he reached Clem's, a dark sedan came toward him. Jeremy recognized it as the first car he had seen going the other way the day before. The sedan stopped in front of Clem's and a woman and a girl got out. The girl seemed to be about Jeremy's age. She looked at him curiously, then followed the woman into the store.

Jeremy went in, too.

The girl stood just inside the door, looking at a rack of greeting cards. She watched Jeremy as he took cans of soup, applesauce, and peaches from the shelves.

Jeremy went to the cooler to see if there were small cartons of milk. There weren't, so he selected a six-pack of canned apple juice. He looked for vegetable seeds, but didn't see any.

As he put his purchases on the counter, the girl said, "Hi. Do you live around here?"

"No, I'm just visiting," Jeremy said.

"Oh, drat. I was hoping you had moved to Lindsburg."

Lindsburg, Jeremy thought. I'm near a town called Lindsburg.

"Is that where you live?" he asked.

"No, but we go there a lot to visit my aunt and uncle. It's the biggest town around here, which isn't saying much, and it is dull beyond belief. Except for seven-year-old twins, there isn't a single kid in town."

"Lindsburg is a charming little city," said the woman. "There's nothing dull about it."

The girl rolled her eyes at Jeremy. "We were just there," she said, "and the big topic of conversation for today is whether it might rain again later in the week."

If they had just come from Lindsburg, Jeremy thought, then Lindsburg was east of Clem's. He wondered how far east. Was it within walking distance?

"I must have been asleep when we drove through Lindsburg," he said. "What's there, besides the twins?"

"A post office," the girl said. "A veterinary office, a bank, and a medical clinic. There's a sec-

ondhand store that's only open in the summer
when people drive to Lake Comstock for the day.
Oh, and Lucky Lindy's, which is kind of an all-
purpose store that sells clothing, food, magazines,
drugstore items, tools, all kinds of stuff."

"Sounds interesting," Jeremy said.

"Lucky Lindy's is fun to browse in," the girl
admitted, "especially if you like fashions from the
fifties."

"I don't know much about fashion," Jeremy
said.

"So I see," the girl replied, as she looked at
Jeremy's torn shirt, which was stained with dirt
and blood. He realized he should have washed the
shirt. It was as dirty as Clem's shirt.

Clem got out of his chair and faced Jeremy
across the counter. "You going to pay for those
groceries or just stand and chitchat all day?" he
asked.

Jeremy took out his money.

"Oh, Clem, don't be such a grouch," the girl
said. "No wonder you don't get many customers."

"Bonnie!" the woman said from the back of the
store. "Mind your manners."

Jeremy smiled at the girl and she smiled back.
She had twinkly brown eyes and sand-colored hair
pulled into a ponytail. When Jeremy carried his
bag of groceries out the door, she followed him.

"Who are you visiting?" the girl asked.

"Nobody," Jeremy said. "My family rented a cabin."

"One of the cabins on Lake Comstock?"

"No. Where's Lake Comstock?"

"About two miles that way." She pointed west. "That's where I live. If you get out that way, our house is the yellow one with the sign in front that says Antiques. I'd love to have company. Lake Comstock isn't quite as boring as Lindsburg, because of the lake, but it isn't exactly New York City. If you've rented a cabin around here, you know what I mean."

He wanted to tell her about the shots he had heard in the night, but if he did that, he would have to tell her where the cabin was.

He knew nothing about this girl; he couldn't tell her about his hideout.

"Where do you go to school?" Jeremy asked.

"I'm homeschooled."

"Do you like that?" He had never known anyone who did not attend public school.

"It's okay, except that I don't meet other kids. We've only lived here a year. After my parents divorced, Mom opened an antiques shop here because her sister lives in Lindsburg. I didn't think she'd get any business clear out in the boonies, but you'd be amazed how many people drive out here to look for bargains. What's your name?"

Jeremy started to say his real name but caught himself just in time. "Joe," he replied. "Joe Edwards."

"I'm Bonnie Tyland. I'll be twelve next week. I like to read, swim, weave baskets out of pine needles, play with my pet owl, ride my bike, make root beer floats, and row our boat around the lake."

"How did you get a pet owl?" Jeremy asked.

"I don't really have an owl." She grinned. "I just put that in to see if you were listening."

Jeremy laughed.

"Mom says I talk so much that people tune me out, so I sometimes test her theory. If I lived in a bigger city," she continued, "I would take ballet and gymnastics, but Mom wants me to grow up where there isn't any violence or bad language. I think she's afraid if we stayed in town and I went to a public school someone might walk in one day and shoot me for no reason. Fat chance."

Memories flooded into Jeremy's mind.

"It happens," he said. He bit his bottom lip and looked away, blinking back sudden tears.

As he struggled to get his emotions under control, Bonnie's mother came out of the store.

"This is my new friend, Joe," Bonnie said. "This is my mom."

Jeremy said, "Hello, Mrs. Tyland."

"Can we give you a ride?" she asked.

"No, thanks. I like to walk."

Mrs. Tyland got in the car. "Let's go," she told Bonnie. "It's time to open the shop."

"Come and visit," Bonnie said as she waved good-bye through the open window. "If it's a hot day, bring your swimsuit. Do you like to play Monopoly? I do. Maybe we could pack a picnic lunch and row out to the island." She was still talking as the car pulled away.

Jeremy walked back to the cabin. He now knew that he was somewhere between Lake Comstock and Lindsburg. He knew there was a store in the region, where he could buy clothes and probably seeds and anything else he needed.

Best of all, he felt he had a friend. Even though he had just met her, and she was a year and a half younger than he was, he liked Bonnie Tyland.

It was good to know someone who lived nearby. He would like to visit her. If they got to be good friends, he might even trust her enough to tell her the truth about who he was and why he was here.

Not too soon, he cautioned himself. Don't give away your secrets until you are positive she won't tell anyone. She's already admitted that her mother thinks she talks too much.

Jeremy reached the footbridge and looked both

ways to be sure no cars were approaching. He didn't want anyone to see where he left the road.

After he put his purchases in the cupboard, he decided to walk to Lake Comstock. He was curious to see where Bonnie lived, and he had discovered that walking helped him forget his problems. It also helped to be physically tired at night, so that he fell asleep quickly.

He returned to the gravel road, and headed west.

He had gone about the length of a city block when he saw dark stains on the shoulder of the road. For an instant, he thought they were oil stains and wondered if a car had broken down there recently.

Then he saw that the stains started just at the edge of the road but continued into the woods.

The weeds and grasses at the edge of the woods near the stains were bent over as if someone had trampled them.

Jeremy crouched and looked closely at the stains. They weren't black, like oil or grease.

He put the tip of his index finger into the largest stain, which was still damp. When he looked at his finger, it was a deep red.

Blood, Jeremy thought. Those stains are blood!

The hair on his arms stood on end. He wiped his finger in the dirt.

He had walked here the day before and had seen

no stains beside the road then. They were so obvious now; he was sure he would have noticed them if they had been here.

Had a car hit a deer or some other animal, and had the animal gone off into the woods leaving a trail of blood? There were no black marks on the road where a car had braked suddenly, and no bloodstains on the road itself, only on the shoulder. If an animal had been struck by a vehicle, there would be brake marks for sure.

Jeremy looked back toward the footbridge. He was close enough to his hideout that if someone fired a gun in this area, he would hear it at the cabin.

The shots he had heard the night before had seemed to come from this direction.

What had happened here? Jeremy wondered. Who had fired a gun last night? What—or who—had been shot?

Because his parents had been so involved in hunting issues, Jeremy knew that some people used lights at night to hunt deer. Although it was illegal, the hunters drove slowly along country roads, beaming bright flashlights into the trees.

When a deer was caught in the spotlight, it would freeze, staring into the light. Standing completely still, the deer made an easy target.

Jeremy wondered if that was what had happened here. He hoped not. It seemed so unfair and cruel. Still, people did poach deer and elk out of season, and they used unlawful methods.

Other possibilities also came to Jeremy's mind. This might not be the blood of a deer or some other animal. What if a person had been shot?

He thought of going on to Bonnie's house and calling the police or sheriff. But if he called the authorities, they would ask his name and address and they might want to speak to his parents. It would be impossible to keep his identity a secret.

Why call the police, he thought, when he did not know if any crime had been committed? Maybe he should just walk on, and pretend he had not seen the stains. He could go to Lake Comstock, maybe even knock on Bonnie's door and visit her, and then walk home on the other side of the road where he wouldn't have to look at the stains.

He remembered Mom saying, "When you ignore a problem, you become part of the problem."

Jeremy decided to look around a bit more. Maybe he would see clues that showed who had been here or what had happened.

Dreading what he might find, Jeremy stepped off the road and followed the patches of stained weeds into the woods.

CHAPTER
10

Jeremy moved slowly, looking for clues. He couldn't tell if someone had walked in the thick undergrowth or not.

Then, near his ankles, he saw drops of dried blood on the leaves of a low shrub. He shuddered as he went past the spots but he kept going, every nerve alert.

He could not move in a straight line, but whoever had been here the night before would not have been able to walk directly in either. There were too many bushes as well as dead trees and fallen branches.

Jeremy stepped around a cedar stump and stopped. Ahead of him on the ground lay the body of a large black bear. The bear's underside had been slit open and its front paws had been cut off. Shocked, Jeremy stared at the carnage.

This bear was bigger than the mother bear he had encountered. Why would anyone kill such a splendid animal and not even use the meat or the fur?

What a waste, Jeremy thought. What a horrible waste! His stomach lurched and Jeremy knew he was going to be sick. Turning away from the bear, he vomited up his breakfast.

He had often heard people say, "It makes me sick," when they disapproved of something. This was the first time the saying had literal meaning for Jeremy.

He wiped his mouth on his sleeve, closed his eyes, and said what his mother had always said when she saw a dead animal alongside the road. "Thank you for your beauty and your spirit. Thank you, bear."

Jeremy looked at the bear again. Surely the animal would not have been killed just to get its claws. The bear claw necklace that Clem had for sale was only five dollars. Jeremy wasn't sure how many claws a bear had on each front paw, but if it was five, that would mean fifty dollars for two paws. Surely nobody would shoot a beautiful creature like this just to get fifty dollars.

Could the bear have attacked someone? Perhaps the person shot it in self-defense. But if that had been the case, the shooter would not have stayed around and cut off the paws. The natural instinct would have been to shoot and run, to get away fast.

And why would the bear's underside be slit open? Although he tried not to look at that part, Jeremy's eyes slid toward the bloody crevice. The sight made him angry.

He no longer felt sick; he felt furious. I'm going to find out who did this, he vowed. I can't do anything to help this bear but I can try to prevent whoever shot him from ever killing another animal illegally.

Jeremy walked slowly around the bear's body, examining every inch of ground. As he did, it occurred to him that the poacher might return. Perhaps the reason the bear's head was not taken as a trophy, or the hide for a rug, was that it got too dark for the killer to work. He may have intended to return to finish the job.

Jeremy stood still, listening. He heard a blue jay call and the rustle of the breeze in the trees but nothing to indicate that a person was nearby.

I'll need to be careful, he thought. I can't let anyone see me come out of the woods near the bloodstains.

He supposed the stains had been made by the bear's paws as they were carried away. Jeremy's anger intensified as he imagined the scene.

On the far side of the bear, near the bloody stump of its front leg, something silver caught Jeremy's attention. He squatted to get a closer look and saw a nickel lying in the dirt. Next to the nickel lay a small scrap of paper.

Jeremy picked up the paper. It was a receipt from Clem's Country Market. Someone had purchased a package of batteries there the day before. No doubt the receipt and the nickel had fallen from the pocket of whoever had shot the bear.

It wasn't Clem, Jeremy thought. If Clem needed batteries, all he had to do was take them. He wouldn't have to buy them from his own store.

Jeremy put the nickel and the receipt in his pocket.

He walked away from the dead bear, wondering what he should do. If he called the game warden or some other law enforcement official, he would have to identify himself, and that would mean leaving his hideout and going to Uncle Ed's now. He didn't want to do that.

Yet he could not ignore what he had found. To do so would go against everything his parents had stood for—all their years of working to have animals treated with respect and kindness. He had to report the bear and tell where it was; if he didn't, the poacher would never be caught.

He heard a car on the road. What if the poacher returned now? Jeremy stood still and listened until the car passed.

At the edge of the woods he proceeded cautiously toward the shoulder of the road, looking back and forth to be sure no cars were approaching. Once on the road, he continued toward Lake Comstock.

As he walked he formed a tentative plan. He would tell Bonnie about the bear and ask her to call the game warden. That way he would not have to give his name, but the poaching would still get reported.

Of course that plan meant that he would have to trust Bonnie not to blab that Jeremy had discovered the bear. It also meant he would have to tell Bonnie why he didn't want to make the call himself. Could he trust her not to tell anyone the truth about his situation?

I have nothing to lose, Jeremy decided. If I tell Bonnie and she doesn't keep it to herself, I'm no worse off than if I call the game warden myself. Doing nothing is not a choice, so I'll just have to take a chance on my new friend.

The road eased downhill shortly before Lake

Comstock came into view. Small homes circled the lake. Several boats bobbed on the water next to wooden docks.

Jeremy spotted the yellow house and walked that way. He knocked on the door, and Bonnie opened it.

"Hi!" she said. "I'm glad you came."

"I need to talk to you," Jeremy said.

"Come on in."

"Could you come out? I don't want anyone else to hear this."

"Oh, goodie, a secret!" Bonnie said. "I love secrets! We can sit down on the dock. Just wait a sec while I tell Mom."

She disappeared into the house and returned a minute later. Jeremy followed her around the side of the house and down a stone path to the water's edge. The wooden dock extended about twelve feet out over the water. A small rowboat was tethered at the end.

Bonnie sat cross-legged on the dock and motioned for Jeremy to sit too. "So what's the secret?" she asked.

"You have to promise not to tell anyone. Not even your mother."

Bonnie's smile faded. "Are you in trouble?" she asked.

"No. But I discovered something that needs to

get reported to the sheriff, and I can't be the one to report it."

"Why not?"

"Promise you won't tell?"

Bonnie thought a moment. "I won't tell as long as we aren't in danger by not telling," she said.

"Fair enough." Jeremy took a deep breath, wondering where to start. "First of all," he said, "my real name is Jeremy Holland. My family didn't rent a cabin; my parents are dead."

"I'm sorry," Bonnie said.

"I walked away from a train wreck and found a cabin, and I'm staying there by myself."

"Were you on the train that crashed? Is that how your parents died?"

"I was on the train, but my parents weren't."

"Were you hurt? Was it really scary? How can you live all alone? Don't you have any other family?"

Jeremy ignored her questions. "On my way here this morning," he said, "I found some bloodstains on the side of the road. I followed the stains into the woods, and I found a dead bear. It had been slit open and its front paws were cut off."

Bonnie's eyes widened and her mouth opened. "How horrible," she said.

"I'm pretty sure hunting isn't legal at this time of year," Jeremy said, "and I want to report what I found, but if I do I'll have to tell the authorities who I am, and they'll make me leave the cabin. I really want to hide out until the end of the summer."

"I think you'd better start at the beginning," Bonnie said. "Tell me exactly who you're hiding from and why you're living alone in the woods."

Jeremy did.

When he had finished, Bonnie said, "Okay. I'll help, and I won't tell on you."

"Thanks. First we need to find out if it's legal to hunt bears now."

"That's easy," Bonnie said. "I'll call Lucky Lindy's and ask. They sell hunting licenses."

They walked back to the house. "Oh, good," Bonnie said, pointing to a car parked in the driveway. "Mom has a customer in the shop. We can use the phone in the kitchen and she won't pay any attention."

Bonnie looked up the number, dialed, and asked if it was legal to hunt black bears now. Then she said, "Can you give me the number to call to report a bear that was killed?"

She listened, scribbled a phone number on the tablet next to the phone, and then listened some more. "Thank you," she said, and hung up.

"No hunting is legal in the spring," she said. "He said there's a suspected bear-poaching operation in this area. The poachers cut the gallbladders out of the bears and sell them to people in Asia. He said the game warden will want to see the bear you found."

"Why would anyone want the gallbladder of a bear?" Jeremy asked. He wasn't even sure what a gallbladder was, except he knew it was an internal organ that people sometimes had to have removed surgically.

"Beats me," Bonnie said. "He gave me the phone number for the game warden's office, but if I call and a game warden comes here, I'll have to tell Mom what's going on."

"Maybe we can meet out on the road, where the stains are," Jeremy suggested.

Bonnie dialed the number. "I want to report that someone shot a bear," she said. She waited a minute and then repeated the statement.

She continued, "It's in the woods just off State Road 213 between Lindsburg and Lake Comstock. If you can meet me there, my friend and I will lead you into the woods and show you where the bear is."

"What did they say?" Jeremy asked after Bonnie had given her name and replaced the receiver.

"The game warden will meet us there in half an hour. You'll have to come, too, because I don't know where the bear is."

She put the game warden's phone number in her jeans pocket, then wrote a note on the tablet: "Mom, my new friend Joe and I have gone for a walk."

"Let's go," she said. "Quick, before Mom's customer leaves. Mom won't care if I go for a walk with you, but she'll ask where we plan to go and I don't want to explain."

Jeremy jogged back up the hill away from Lake Comstock, with Bonnie trotting beside him. He had no trouble finding the stains on the side of the road.

"I hope the game warden comes right away," he said. "I get nervous standing here. What if the poacher returns?"

"If anyone else stops," Bonnie said, "we'll stroll away as if we're just out for a walk."

Bonnie sounded unconcerned, but dozens of what-if's flew through Jeremy's head. What if the poacher didn't believe them? What if he followed them? What if he threatened them?

CHAPTER
11

Jeremy quit worrying when a Department of Wildlife car approached. Bonnie waved. The car pulled to a stop next to the kids; then a game warden and a sheriff got out.

"Are you the one who called about a bear?" the game warden asked.

"Yes," Bonnie said.

"It's in the woods," Jeremy said, "this way." He led the way through the undergrowth.

Bonnie gasped when she saw the bear.

"Greed," said the game warden. "That's what's behind this: greed."

"Mr. Lindy told us the bear's gallbladder gets sold," Bonnie said. "Is that true?"

"That's right. Bear gallbladders bring several

hundred dollars on the black market. They're used in Asian folk medicine as a remedy for many ailments. The poachers usually sell other body parts, too."

The sheriff added, "The paws are used for soup or made into ashtrays, and the claws are used for necklaces. Sometimes the teeth are removed and sometimes the skin is made into a rug, but usually the carcass is left to rot. The poachers don't want to get caught, so they work fast and run."

"I hope you kids didn't go any closer," the game warden said.

"I did," Jeremy admitted. "I walked all around the bear, looking for clues to who might have shot him."

The men looked unhappy. "Walking around like that contaminates a crime scene," the sheriff said. "Now we won't be able to get clear footprints."

"I'm sorry," Jeremy said. "I didn't know." He added, "I found a receipt for batteries, from Clem's Country Market, and I found this nickel, too." He handed over the nickel and the receipt. "They were on the ground right next to the bear."

"It's too bad you touched them," said the sheriff. "We might have gotten fingerprints."

Jeremy felt embarrassed that he had been so stupid. "I'm sorry," he said again. "I didn't think of that."

"In a poaching case," the game warden said, "we look for anything that doesn't grow naturally in the area. If it doesn't grow there, it's a clue."

"How did you happen to find the bear?" the sheriff asked.

"I was camping out in the woods last night," Jeremy said, "and I heard shots, just before dark. This morning I saw those stains by the side of the road and went to investigate. After I found the bear, I went to Bonnie's house and we called you from there."

"Did you see or hear anything else unusual, either last night or today?"

Jeremy shook his head.

"Clem sells bear claw necklaces," Bonnie said.

"Who?"

"Clem. Up the road at Clem's Country Market. He has bear claw necklaces for five dollars each."

"There's only one necklace there now," Jeremy said. "He offered it to me for four-fifty."

The game warden took photos of the bear.

"We want you kids to stay out of these woods," the sheriff said. "People who kill animals illegally are not hunters; they are thieves. They steal wildlife and sell the parts for their own personal gain. Like any other thieves, they can be extremely dangerous if they think they're going to get caught. So stay away from here and don't talk to anyone except your parents about this. We have a better chance of catching the poacher if he doesn't know we're looking for him."

Jeremy and Bonnie followed the two men back to the road.

"Can we give you kids a ride home?" the game warden asked.

"No, thanks." Bonnie and Jeremy answered at the same time.

"Remember what we said," the sheriff warned. "Stay out of the woods around here until this case is solved."

Jeremy watched the car make a U-turn and drive back the way it had come.

"I wonder if they'll stop at Clem's," Bonnie said, "and ask him if he remembers who bought batteries recently."

Jeremy didn't answer her. He wasn't thinking about Clem; he was thinking about himself. The sheriff had said to stay away from these woods, but how could he? His cabin was in the forest.

He wondered just how dangerous the poacher might be.

"Let's go home and look up poaching on the Internet," Bonnie said.

"Do you have a computer?" Jeremy asked. "And Internet access?"

"Don't look so shocked. We may live out in the

country, but we still have electricity and a telephone line. This *is* the twenty-first century, you know."

"That's one of the things I've missed most," Jeremy said. "I used to play card games on the computer, and my friend Paul and I sent e-mail to each other."

Thinking of Paul made Jeremy feel guilty. By now Paul probably believed that Jeremy had died in the train wreck. Jeremy knew how unhappy he would feel if he thought Paul had been killed. He was sorry that his friend was experiencing such terrible grief.

Jeremy wished he could send Paul an e-mail, saying that he was alive and well, that he was hiding out for a few weeks before he went to Chicago. But he knew that e-mail could be traced, just as phone calls could. In spite of his remorse and his uneasiness about staying in his hideout with a poacher nearby, he wasn't ready to call Uncle Ed.

"Mom's always telling me to use the Internet to do research," Bonnie said. "I think she wants to be sure we get our money's worth from the online service every month."

Back at Bonnie's house, she took two apples from a bowl and handed one to Jeremy. The computer was in one corner of the living room. Bonnie logged on and then did a search for "bear poaching."

Jeremy read over her shoulder as pages of information appeared.

"Wow," Bonnie said. "It looks as if poaching bears is more common than we thought. Bear parts get sold in lots of Asian countries."

"If the market for bear parts is in Asia," Jeremy said, "why are the poachers shooting bears here? Aren't there any bears in Asia?"

A few minutes later the answer to his question appeared as Bonnie scrolled down the information on the screen.

"Bears have become rare in Asia," Jeremy read aloud, "so the wholesale market now is in North America."

"Wholesale!" Bonnie sputtered. "They make it sound as if the bears are pottery or wood instead of living creatures. Wholesale means that a middleman is getting a cut of the profits."

"First there's the poacher," Jeremy said, "who sells the gallbladder to a wholesaler, who sells it to a retailer, who sells it to the final customer. That means at least three people are making money from each bear."

"This whole thing burns me up," Bonnie said. "When the sheriff said the bear paws sometimes get made into ashtrays, I just wanted to scream."

She got up and stomped around the room as if she needed to kick something. "Ashtrays!" she said. "It's bad enough that people still smoke, but to use those impressive big paws for ashtrays is just—"

Jeremy interrupted her. "Listen to this," he said as he continued to read from the computer screen. "Hundreds of American bears are killed and the parts smuggled into Asia each year. Wholesalers get as much as five thousand dollars for one American bear."

"That," said Bonnie, "is totally disgusting. I hope they catch the person who is killing bears around here."

"I wonder what the penalty is for bear poaching."

Bonnie put both hands on her hips and made an angry face. "They should cut off the poacher's hands and make them into ashtrays," she said. "It would serve him right."

Shocked, Jeremy stared at her.

"Oh, I don't really mean that," Bonnie said. "But I hope he doesn't get let off with a tiny fine that isn't half the amount of money that he makes from one bear. I hope he gets put in jail."

"So do I."

Bonnie's mother came in. "What are you doing?" she asked.

"We're learning about wildlife poaching," Bonnie said. "When we were out walking, we saw a Department of Wildlife car parked along the road. The game warden and the sheriff were there because someone had shot a bear illegally."

That's true, Jeremy thought. Everything she said is true.

"I hope you stayed out of their way," Mrs. Tyland said.

"We didn't bother them," Bonnie said, "but now we're learning about poachers."

"The poacher probably wanted the bear's gallbladder," Mrs. Tyland said.

Bonnie and Jeremy both looked surprised.

"How do you know that?" Bonnie asked.

"Your dear old mom knows lots of things."

Jeremy grinned. That was exactly the kind of remark *his* mom used to make.

"There have been rumors of a poaching ring around here for a long time," Mrs. Tyland added.

"I thought we moved out to the country to get away from crime," Bonnie said.

"There are problems anywhere there are people," Mrs. Tyland said. "Let's talk about something more cheerful, such as the fact that the pizza I put in the oven is ready to eat."

"That sounds great," Bonnie said. "I'm starving."

"Can you stay and eat with us, Joe?" Mrs. Tyland asked.

"I'd love to," Jeremy said. After four days of eating cold beans, burned soup, and peanut butter sandwiches, the smell of hot pizza made his mouth water.

After they had eaten, Mrs. Tyland told Bonnie that she needed to do her arithmetic and study her spelling words.

Bonnie wrinkled up her nose. "Do I have to do it right this minute?" she asked. "I hardly ever have company."

"Joe can come again tomorrow," Mrs. Tyland said. "If you had done your schoolwork first thing this morning, as I asked you to, you wouldn't have to do it now."

"I'll walk him out to the road," Bonnie said.

Jeremy thanked Mrs. Tyland for the pizza and left, with Bonnie beside him.

As soon as the door closed behind them, Bonnie whispered, "Where will you go?"

"Back to the cabin."

"But you can't! The sheriff told us to stay out of the woods. It's too dangerous for you to live there by yourself."

"I don't have anyplace else to go."

CHAPTER
12

You could hide in our garage," Bonnie suggested. "I'll sneak you food."

"No. I'd be seen, or your mom would catch on, and then you'd be in trouble."

"I don't want you to stay in that cabin alone. What if the poacher shoots you?"

"I'm not a bear. My gallbladder isn't worth five thousand dollars, so why would anyone shoot me?"

Bonnie stopped walking. "Wait here," she said, then turned and ran back toward the house. A minute later she returned, carrying a cellular telephone.

"Here," she said, handing him the phone. "Mom keeps this in her purse, in case we ever have car trouble or an accident or a medical emergency. You take it. That way you can call for help if you need to."

"Won't your mom miss this?"

"Not unless our car breaks down. We've had the phone over a year and we've only used it once, when we were on our way to my aunt's house in Lindsburg and there was an accident ahead of us and the road was closed. Mom says cell calls are too expensive, so we use it only for emergencies."

Jeremy longed to take the phone, but he shook his head. "It's nice of you to offer," he said, "but I can't take that."

"Why not?"

"Because if you and your mom had an emergency while I had your cell phone, I'd feel terrible."

"You're more likely to need it in the next few days than we are," Bonnie said.

Jeremy hoped she was wrong about that.

"Come back tomorrow," Bonnie said. "I'll get up early and do all my schoolwork before you get here. We won't talk about bear poachers or anything else horrible. Maybe Mom will let us make cookies. What kind do you like best?"

Jeremy started to say snickerdoodles, but Bonnie kept right on talking.

"My favorites are chocolate-chip with nuts, and

plain sugar cookies," she said. "Do you like to play Clue? That's my favorite game. I always guess that Professor Plum did it with a lead pipe in the library. Do you know how to swim? I just learned how to do a back dive off the dock, but I'm not allowed to do it unless Mom is watching. Will you come tomorrow?"

"Yes," Jeremy said. "See you then."

"You're sure you don't want the phone?"

"I'm sure."

He started to walk on, then stopped when Bonnie called his name.

He looked back at her.

"Be careful."

"I will."

When Jeremy reached the footbridge, he did not return to his hideout. He was reluctant to go back to the cabin, so he kept walking until he reached Clem's.

As soon as he went inside the store, Clem got out of his chair and said, "If you came back to buy the necklace, you're too late. I sold it this morning. Got the full five dollars for it."

Jeremy could tell that Clem was hoping Jeremy would be disappointed.

"My dad said I couldn't have it," Jeremy said.

"Too bad," Clem said. "That necklace was a real bargain."

Jeremy wanted to ask who had purchased the necklace. Maybe the game warden had bought it so that they could prove Clem sold such items.

Jeremy took a box of doughnuts off the shelf. Bonnie's talk about cookies had made him hungry for something sweet.

"Yep," Clem said, "a fellow walked in here, spotted that necklace, and bought it, just like that. Never quibbled about the price at all. He knew it was a steal." He started chuckling, as if he had just told a joke.

"Steal" was the right word, Jeremy thought, only not the way Clem meant it. The sheriff had said poachers were thieves.

He put the doughnuts on the counter by the cash register and took two dollars from his wallet.

Clem kept chuckling.

"You want to hear the best part of all?" Clem asked.

"Sure." Jeremy suspected he was the first customer through the door since the necklace had been sold, and he could tell Clem was bursting to tell what had happened.

"The dude who bought it was a cop! A sheriff!"

Jeremy pretended to be astonished. "No kidding!" he said.

"Don't that beat all?" Clem said. "A cop bought my bear claw necklace!"

You don't know the half of it, Jeremy thought. Clem had obviously failed to notice the Department of Wildlife car and the game warden who drove it.

Clem kept laughing while he gave Jeremy his change. Jeremy pretended to laugh too.

"It's the best thing that's happened in weeks," Clem said.

"I wonder why the sheriff was here," Jeremy said.

"He was looking for speeders."

Jeremy wondered if Clem was guessing or if that was what the sheriff had told him.

Listening to Clem gloat over the sale of the necklace convinced Jeremy that Clem was not the poacher. The person who had shot the bears and sold the paws and other parts had to know enough not to talk about it. When it came to making money, Jeremy didn't think Clem would be able to keep his mouth shut for five minutes. If Clem had poached any bears, he would have been caught long ago.

"Where did you get the necklace?" Jeremy asked.

Clem scratched his head, as if trying to remember. Then he said, "I bought four of them last year from a guy whose wife made them. Don't know where they got the claws. I kept one of the necklaces for myself and sold the others." He started to laugh again. "Doubled my money," he said. "I paid two bucks apiece."

Clem was still chortling as Jeremy carried his doughnuts out the door.

He stayed inside for the rest of the day, reading one of his books. Every half hour or so he went to the windows and looked out, hoping he would not see anyone.

The woods were silent. As daylight changed to dusk, Jeremy saw an owl fly across the clearing, silent as a ghost. When the last shadow faded to darkness, he went to bed, but he had a hard time falling asleep. He wished he had Bonnie's cellular telephone under his pillow. Several times during the night, he jerked awake, imagining that he had heard voices outside.

Maybe it was a mistake to try to spend the summer here, he thought. He had expected that staying in the cabin would help him feel calm and peaceful, the way he had always felt on the camping trips with Mom and Dad. Instead, the dead bear made him feel vulnerable, as if all his troubles had followed him into the forest.

CHAPTER

13

Arnie Cotton drove around the block twice. Finally, on the third trip, there were no cars nearby when he reached the entrance to the alley behind the office building.

He turned off his car lights just before he pulled into the alley. Then he eased the vehicle forward until he was beside the third back door.

Leaving the engine running, he dialed a number on his cell phone.

"I'm here," he said.

Seconds later the door opened, and a man slipped out into the darkness.

Arnie got out, lifted the insulated box from the seat beside him, and handed it to the man. "One gallbladder," he said softly, "and two paws."

The man handed Arnie an envelope in exchange for the box.

Arnie looked inside, but it was too dark to tell if all the money was there.

"You can count it, if you like."

"It's always been the right amount before."

"You'll make another delivery soon?"

The question irritated Arnie. He did all the hard part while this guy sat in his office demanding more and more.

"Some kids found this bear's carcass," Arnie said, "and called the cops."

The man stiffened. "How do you know that?" he asked. "Were you questioned?" He looked both ways down the dark alley. "You aren't being followed, are you?"

"Naw, they don't suspect me. My sister-in-law is doing a temporary job at the county sheriff's office, and she overhears a lot. She told me about the kids."

"The kids must live near where you shot the bear. You should hunt somewhere else."

Who are you to tell me where to hunt? Arnie thought. He said, "Those kids are spooked. They won't go back into the woods."

"What about the sheriff? Did you pick up the shotgun shell cases? You didn't leave anything behind, did you?"

"Cops have more pressing problems to deal with. A couple of bear hunters way out in the boonies are not going to attract their attention."

"If you ever get caught," the man said, "and you try to link me to this, I'll deny it." He opened the door.

"I won't get caught. Me and Jeff are going back tomorrow morning. We need to get one more bear before Friday, to make enough money for our car payments. Then we'll lay low for a couple of weeks."

"Call me when you have the bear."

"The price is going up."

"How much?"

"Six hundred, instead of five. That's to make up for the extra risk of having the cops know about this one."

"What extra risk? You just said yourself they can't be bothered."

"Six hundred," Arnie repeated.

"For that much money, you'll have to bring all four paws."

"I'll try. It got dark on me this time, and it's too risky to use a flashlight."

"Hunt earlier," the man said, "and don't let any kids see you." He carried the box inside, shutting the door behind him.

Arnie glared after him. Easy for him to say, he

thought. Mr. fancy-schmancy medical man sits in his nice safe office while I risk my tail hunting bears. Next time I ought to charge him seven hundred. See how he likes that!

Still grumbling to himself, Arnie pulled out of the alley and headed home. Those kids had better not come snooping around again, he thought. If they do, they'll regret it.

Jeremy woke early and watched the room gradually grow light. He dressed, made a fire, and heated potato soup in the kettle. He remembered a camping trip when he had eaten potato soup for breakfast with his parents. That time the soup had been accompanied by thick slices of whole wheat bread, toasted over the fire. After they ate, Jeremy had roasted marshmallows on a stick and made s'mores, declaring that he could have dessert with breakfast, since he was on vacation.

So many memories, Jeremy thought, as he brushed tears from his eyes. For the rest of my life, little things like potato soup will bring a flood of memories.

Despite the ache of missing his parents, he felt more optimistic than he had the night before. He was eager to go to Bonnie's house and find out if the sheriff or the game warden had called to say they had caught the poacher.

After he had eaten, he refilled the clean kettle with water and put it back on the fire. When the water was warm, he took the kettle off the fire and removed his shirt.

Mrs. Tyland had glanced at his filthy shirt more than once yesterday. If he continued to wear the same shirt without washing it, she might start asking questions.

He dipped the slim bar of soap into the kettle and scrubbed his shirt with it, rubbing all the dirtiest spots. Then he swished the shirt back and forth in the water. He could hardly believe how dark the water got.

He emptied the kettle and then pumped it full again. It took four rinses before the water stayed clear, and even then his shirt still had some stains.

At least I won't stink, Jeremy thought as he wrung water out of the shirt. He held the shirt close to the fire to dry it, staying on the side away from the smoke.

One day soon he wanted to go to Lindsburg. He planned to buy a new shirt, extra underwear, and socks at Lucky Lindy's. Maybe he could get a ride the next time Bonnie and her mother went.

Jeremy grew bored with waiting for his shirt to dry so he put it on while it was still damp. He left the fire burning low, so he wouldn't have to start it again to heat his lunch, then went inside to wait until it was late enough to go to Bonnie's house.

He picked up the book he was reading, sat on the bed, and stared at the page, unable to concentrate. He felt edgy and restless.

Arnie stood at his window, watching for Jeff's pickup. What was keeping him? They had agreed to leave by eight and it was already past eight-thirty.

He hoped that jalopy of Jeff's hadn't refused to run. Usually Arnie drove on their hunting trips. His SUV was newer than Jeff's truck and more dependable. If they ever needed to get away in a hurry, Arnie's vehicle was the better choice.

Last night, after they divided the money, however, they had agreed that Jeff would drive today, just in case anyone had noticed Arnie's SUV parked at the edge of the woods yesterday. The game warden might question local people; it would be best to leave Arnie's vehicle at home, where it would not be recognized.

"You drive," Arnie had said, "and we'll go in at a different place. Instead of parking along the edge of the road, we'll take that old logging road that heads into the woods just before Lake Comstock. We'll drive in as far as we can and leave your truck where it's not visible from the road."

"There's no gas in my truck," Jeff had said. "I ran short of cash."

Arnie pointed to the five twenty-dollar bills on Jeff's table. "You aren't short of cash now," he said.

Jeff smiled. "That's right," he said. "I can buy gas before I pick you up."

He probably forgot, Arnie thought as he waited, or else he didn't have enough gas in the tank to make it to a station.

Sometimes he wondered why he continued to be partners with Jeff. It wasn't because of Jeff's brains, that was certain. He worried about what would happen if they ever got caught. He had told Jeff a dozen times exactly what he should say if anyone ever found them killing a bear out of season: "It attacked us! We had to shoot it in self-defense." Yet he knew Jeff was just as likely to make up some implausible story or, worse yet, to blurt out the truth.

Still, there were two things in Jeff's favor. First, he was a great shot, usually bringing down the bear on the first try. Second, he was too stupid to find out how much Arnie really received for the bear parts. When Arnie told Jeff that he got two hundred dollars per bear, Jeff was happy to get his half. He never checked up on Arnie, to see if that was the right amount.

Arnie glanced at his watch again. Eight forty-five. If Jeff didn't get here soon, he would have to go looking for him.

Just then the old tan-and-brown pickup rattled around the corner. Arnie grabbed his gun, walked to the curb, and climbed in.

"You want to stop somewhere for breakfast first?" Jeff asked. "I'm hungry."

Arnie shook his head. "We're already late. We aren't stopping for breakfast."

"Late for what?" Jeff said. "Did you make an appointment with that bear?" He laughed at his own joke, slapping his thigh with one hand and steering with the other.

"The later it gets," Arnie said, "the more likely there will be other people on the road—people who can identify your truck if they're asked."

"You're making me nervous," Jeff said. "Maybe we shouldn't go back so close to where we were last time. What if those same kids see us?"

"They won't."

"But what if they do?"

"Look," Arnie said. "We're going to the same place because we know there's another bear there. We both saw the second one run off the other night."

"If you weren't such a rotten shot," Jeff grumbled, "we'd have had both of them in one night."

"It was too dark. That's why I missed it."

"I didn't miss mine."

"Okay! So I missed. I also got you-know-who to pay us more for this one."

"You did?" Jeff grinned. "How much more?"

"Three hundred," Arnie said. "You're getting a raise, pal, an extra fifty bucks."

"You do good work, Arnie."

"I know."

Half an hour later they parked the truck on the old logging road.

"I remembered to bring bags this time," Jeff said. He removed some large plastic bags from under the seat.

"Good. I ruined a pair of jeans last time because blood dripped all over them."

The two men started into the woods, toward where they had seen the second bear.

They had hunted for only twenty minutes when Arnie said, "I smell smoke."

Both men stopped walking and sniffed the air.

"I smell it, too," Jeff said.

"We need to find where it's coming from."

They walked quietly, listening and watching.

"Look!" Jeff said, pointing through the trees. "There's a fire next to that old cabin. Someone must be staying there."

The two men peered toward the cabin.

"We never saw anyone in that cabin before," Jeff went on.

Arnie put a finger to his lips, signaling Jeff to be quiet. Then he pointed at the woods on the opposite side of the cabin.

A young girl had just emerged from a narrow path. She went straight to the door of the cabin and knocked.

"It's those kids who found the bear," Arnie whispered. "I'd lay money on it. They're playing in that old cabin."

"We can't shoot with them around," Jeff said. "They'll hear us. We'll have to hunt somewhere else."

"No," Arnie said. "I'm not letting two kids chase us out of here. I'll guard the cabin while you hunt. If I hear you shoot, I'll make sure the kids don't leave. After you load the bear parts into the truck, come back here and call me. Don't use my name, just yell, 'All done!' We'll have plenty of time to get away before the kids can run home and tell anyone."

"They'll see you. They'll know what you look like."

"They'll be too scared to give a good description, and after we get the money tonight, you and I will both stay away from here."

"You're a smart man, Arnie."

"I know."

Arnie stayed in the trees, circling to the side of the cabin. He positioned himself where he could see the door.

Jeff walked quietly on, stalking his prey.

Arnie waited. Thinking about those kids made his blood boil. He and Jeff had a good deal going here. What right did those kids have to spoil it? The more he thought about them, the angrier he became.

CHAPTER
14

*K*nock-knock-knock.

Jeremy jumped and dropped his book. He had not heard anyone approach the cabin.

He tiptoed to the window and peeked out, trying to see who was at the door.

Knock-knock-knock.

"Jeremy? Are you there?"

"Bonnie!" Jeremy opened the door. "I didn't hear you coming."

She went inside. "Of course not. I was trying to be quiet in case the poachers were in the woods."

"Did the sheriff or the game warden call?"

"No."

"Then what are you doing here?"

"I got tired of waiting for you. I imagined all sorts of terrible things."

"It's only ten o'clock. I thought you needed to do your schoolwork, so I was going to wait until this afternoon."

"I got up at six. Did they come back last night? Did you hear any more shots?"

"No."

"Whew. I worried about you all night. Well, not quite all night. I used the computer until almost eleven because Mom said since I'm interested in wildlife poaching I can write a report about that, so I looked up some more stuff on the Internet and you won't believe what I found out."

"What?"

"Bears have even been shot within the boundaries of Great Smoky Mountains National Park, and Yellowstone, and some of our other national parks!"

"You're kidding," Jeremy said.

"I wish I were."

"How do the poachers get away with that?"

"They do it at night, sometimes right in the campgrounds and picnic areas or alongside the roads. The federal fish and game officers finally started setting up surprise roadblocks. That's the only way they can catch the poachers. Of course, the more I read, the more I worried about you."

"It was quiet here last night," Jeremy said.

"Good. I hope it stays that way. You washed your shirt."

"I don't want your mother to think I'm a bum."

"But you *are* a bum." She grinned at him.

"Thanks a lot."

"You didn't tell your mom about my cabin, did you?"

Bonnie looked insulted. "Of course not. Mom thinks I walked to Clem's to buy a notebook. She has a customer coming to get a full set of Redwing pottery that he looked at yesterday, and she's so excited about the sale that she hardly listened when I told her I was leaving."

"It probably wasn't too smart to come," Jeremy said, "but I'm glad you did."

Bang!

Jeremy and Bonnie froze.

Bang! Bang! Bang!

These shots were much closer to the cabin than the ones Jeremy had heard before.

"They're back," Bonnie said, her eyes wide. "The poachers are out there."

"We need to get out of here," Jeremy whispered.

"Are you crazy? I'm not walking through that door when someone is out there firing a gun."

"If we run for help right now, the sheriff or

114

game warden might get here in time to catch the poacher in the act. If we wait, he will probably get away."

"What if the poacher sees us?" Bonnie asked.

"If he just shot an animal, he's busy dealing with that. He won't be looking at anything else."

"What if he missed? What if he comes this way? Those shots were close! The shooter is almost certain to see the cabin."

"All the more reason to run for it. If he comes in and finds us here, we have no place to hide and no way to escape."

Bonnie frantically looked around the small room.

"We don't want to get trapped in here," Jeremy said.

"He isn't after us," Bonnie said. "Even if he finds us here, why would he care?"

"Because if we see him, we can identify him. Remember what the sheriff said: he isn't a hunter, he's a thief."

"I hope the sheriff and the game warden catch this crook," Bonnie said.

"They can't catch him if they don't know he's here."

Bonnie followed Jeremy to the door.

He cracked it open and peered out. "I don't see anyone," he whispered. "The shots came from that way." He nodded toward his right. "We'll go down the trail the other way, to the road. We can run to Clem's and call from there."

"I'm scared," Bonnie said. "What if he sees us running and shoots?"

"I'm scared, too," Jeremy admitted, although he thought it was less dangerous to run than to stay where they were. "Think about the bears," he said. "They can't speak for themselves. If we don't help them, who will?"

Jeremy pushed the door open and stepped out onto the porch with Bonnie beside him. They listened, but heard nothing.

"Let's go," Jeremy whispered. Together they rushed off the porch and across the clearing toward the trail.

"Hold it right there!"

The voice came from around the side of the cabin.

Jeremy and Bonnie turned to face a large man wearing a camouflage jacket and hat and holding a gun. Jeremy didn't know anything about guns, but the weapon the man held was long and ominous-looking, and it was pointed straight at Jeremy.

"What's your rush?" the man said.

Jeremy thought fast. "Our dad's waiting to give us a ride to Lindsburg," he said. "We're late."

The man scowled. "I don't believe you," he

said. "If your dad was waiting and he heard gun-fire, he would have come in here looking for you." He motioned with the gun toward the cabin. "Get back inside," he said.

"We don't care if you hunt around here," Jeremy said as they headed back to the cabin with the man behind them.

"Maybe you don't care," the man said, "but you'll blab it to someone who does. Like the cops."

"What do you mean?" Bonnie asked.

The kids stepped inside. The man followed and shut the door.

"My sister-in-law works as a messenger for the county sheriff," he said. "She overhears a lot when she's delivering packages. She tipped me off that the cops were out here looking for poachers, because two kids found a dead bear and reported it."

"I don't know anything about that," Jeremy said.

"Neither do I," Bonnie said.

"Of course not," the man said. "It seems odd to me that two kids are in a cabin not far from where the cops were called, and then those two kids run like their pants are on fire when they hear gun-shots. But of course you would never call the cops again, would you?"

"We didn't call them yesterday either," Bonnie said.

"I never said it was yesterday," the man said.

Bonnie looked panicky.

Jeremy's palms began to sweat. "What are you going to do with us?" he asked.

"I'm going to stay here until my partner finishes up some work out there."

His partner. So there was another man in the woods. And his work was probably the result of shooting another bear.

"Then what?" Bonnie asked.

"Then he and I will decide what to do with you. Now sit down and be quiet."

Jeremy and Bonnie sat on the chairs. The man stood near the window, staring out. Jeremy's mind raced, trying to figure out some way to escape before the man's partner, who no doubt also had a weapon, came into the cabin.

Bonnie began wiggling around in her chair. She crossed and uncrossed her legs. She kept looking hard at Jeremy, obviously trying to relay a message by mental telepathy, but he had no idea what she wanted him to know.

The man turned away from the window and watched Bonnie fidgeting. "Sit still," he said. "You're getting on my nerves."

"I have to go to the bathroom."

"You'll have to wait."

"I can't! I need to go really bad."

"Is there a pot in here?"

"No," Bonnie said. "We just walk down the path a ways and go in the woods." She pointed toward the road.

After she spoke, Bonnie looked at Jeremy again. He could tell from her expression that she was trying to trick the man into letting her leave the cabin. Jeremy hoped she did not intend to run for it.

Bonnie stood up. "I can't wait any longer," she said.

The man looked around the cabin, then pointed to the kettle. "You can use that," he said.

Bonnie wrinkled her nose in disgust. "Yuck!" she said. "That's our cooking pot. I can't use our cooking pot as a toilet."

"You can if you're desperate enough," the man said.

"No, I can't. My mother would have a fit. Besides, I can't go in front of you two. I need some privacy."

The man glared at Bonnie for a moment. She hopped back and forth from one foot to the other. The man sighed and said, "Oh, all right. Go outside. But be quick about it, and come right back."

"Yes," Jeremy said. "Come right back." He emphasized each word, trying to tell Bonnie not to try to escape. It was too risky to run from this man, who was armed.

Bonnie ignored him. She went out the door and trotted toward the path that led to the road.

The man stepped out onto the porch to watch her, leaving the door open.

Jeremy also stood and watched.

When Bonnie left the clearing and entered the path, the man called, "That's far enough!"

Bonnie bolted.

The man swore and started toward the path, glancing once over his shoulder to be sure Jeremy was still inside.

This is my chance, Jeremy thought. He ran to the window at the back of the cabin and then slid it open. He didn't like to leave Bonnie behind, especially now that she had angered the man, but he couldn't help her by staying here.

He climbed through the window and dropped to the ground. He pulled the window shut so it would not be obvious which way he had gone. Then he ran into the forest behind the cabin.

He would have to make his way through the woods. Jeremy knew the road curved, so if he went at an angle to the path, he would join the road partway between the footbridge and Clem's.

He wished he knew exactly where the poacher's accomplice was.

From the front of the cabin, he heard the man shout, "Come back here!"

Good, Jeremy thought. He's still outside. He doesn't know yet that I've left.

"Come back or I'll shoot!" the man yelled.

Go back, Bonnie, Jeremy thought. Go back before you get yourself killed.

Bang!

The sound turned Jeremy's blood to ice water. It had come from the front of the cabin, from where the man was yelling at Bonnie.

CHAPTER

15

Jeremy stopped. He wanted to go back to try to help Bonnie.

Instead, he plunged deeper into the trees. Going back now wouldn't do Bonnie any good. Her only hope was for Jeremy to get away and call for help.

As he ran, he listened for another shot. If the man had missed her the first time, he might fire again.

The second shot did not come.

Thorny shrubs snagged his shirt and left long scratches on his arms. Low-hanging tree branches whipped his face. Twice he tripped on fallen branches and nearly fell, but he did not slow down. He plunged through the woods, caring only about getting help as quickly as possible.

This is all my fault, he thought. I should not have told Bonnie about my hideout. I should never have stayed here to begin with. I not only put myself in danger but I risked my friend's life as well.

Fear propelled him forward long after his breath began coming in painful gasps.

At last he saw a clearing through the trees. He burst out of the woods and onto the edge of the road. Hoping to see a car that he could flag down, he looked quickly in both directions, but the road was deserted. He raced to his left, toward Clem's.

His feet pounded the gravel road as he wiped his sweaty forehead on the hem of his shirt. *Faster!* he told himself. *Run faster!*

When he finally reached Clem's Country Market, he took the steps in one leap and burst through the door yelling, "Clem! I need help!"

Startled, Clem jumped to his feet.

"Call the sheriff!" Jeremy said. "Hurry!"

"Why? What happened?"

"There are two men in the woods. They're bear poachers, and I think one of them shot Bonnie!"

Clem stared at Jeremy with his mouth hanging open, but he made no move.

"We have to get help!" Jeremy said. "Where's your phone?"

Clem still didn't speak, but he glanced at the counter to his left, behind the candy jars, and then looked back at Jeremy.

Jeremy leaned across the counter and looked behind the candy jars. He saw a telephone and reached for it.

Just as Jeremy grabbed the phone, Clem's hand shot out. He pinched the end of the telephone cord to disconnect it, yanked the cord out of the back of the phone, and shoved it in his pocket. Jeremy had the phone, but he could not make a call.

"What are you doing?" Jeremy said. "Don't you understand? Those poachers are in the woods right now. They threatened me and my friend with a gun, and now I think they've shot her."

"It ain't my concern," Clem said.

Jeremy stared at Clem in disbelief. "You aren't going to let me call for help?"

"I don't want any cops swarming around here."

"You were happy enough to see a cop when he bought your necklace."

"That was before I knew why he wanted it. I didn't know he was trying to link me up with a poaching ring."

"What makes you think he is?"

"Because he came back later, with the game warden, and they asked me a bunch of questions. They told me that if I wouldn't help them catch the poachers I might be arrested. I said I ain't no snitch. I ain't no poacher, neither, so they can't be arresting me. If the cops want to catch somebody they can do it on their own, without any help from Clem."

Jeremy's mind raced as he tried to think how he could persuade Clem to let him use the telephone. "If that man shot Bonnie, and if she dies because you wouldn't let me use your telephone, you'll be considered an accomplice in a murder. Do you want to go to jail for aiding in a murder?"

"Murder!" The color drained out of Clem's face. Then he narrowed his eyes and looked hard at Jeremy. "I didn't shoot her. You're just trying to scare me. You don't know for sure that anybody shot her."

"But what if he did?" Jeremy said. "Bonnie was running away from him. She could identify him. He was plenty angry, and I know he fired the gun because I heard the shot." He put the phone down where Clem could reach it. "Please, Clem! Put the cord back in. She could be bleeding to death while we stand here arguing."

Just then Jeremy heard a car coming along the road. He twirled around, opened the door, and stepped outside as the car sped past the store. He heard music coming from inside the car.

"Help!" Jeremy yelled. He ran down the steps and raced after the car, waving his arms and hoping the driver might glance in the rearview mirror. "Stop!" he yelled. "Come back!"

The car kept going.

Tears stung Jeremy's eyes, and he choked on the dust that rose behind the vanishing car. If he didn't get a ride, it would take him nearly an hour to walk all the way to Lake Comstock, and on the way there he would have to pass the footbridge and the path to his cabin. By now, the men were surely looking for him. If they saw him, they would . . .

No, he thought. I can't waste time thinking about what could happen.

He turned to go back inside to plead with Clem one last time. As he went up the steps, Clem shoved the door shut.

Jeremy heard a click as the bolt slid into place, locking the door from the inside. Then he saw the bright red Open sign flip over to Closed.

He felt like flinging a rock through the front window of the store, but he remembered his parents saying, as they watched television reports of rioters and looters, "It's okay to disagree with the law, but it isn't okay to break the law. You have to respect other people and their property."

Jeremy cupped his hands around his eyes and peered through the window. Clem stood just inside the door, looking at him.

"Clem," Jeremy said, "if you let me use your phone, I'll tell the cops you helped me; I'll make you look real good."

Clem said nothing.

"If you don't let me use it," Jeremy continued, "the cops will believe that you were in on the poaching ring. They'll think you wouldn't let me call for help because you wanted to give your partners time to get away."

"That ain't true," Clem said.

"Maybe not, but that's what everyone will think. You sold a bear claw necklace to the sheriff just yesterday."

Clem scratched his head.

"You've got five seconds to open this door, Clem. If you don't, I'll hitchhike to town with the next car that comes by, and when I get there you'll be in deep, deep trouble, and not just because of the poaching. Don't forget that murder charge."

Jeremy held his breath, hoping he had sounded convincing.

Clem turned his back on Jeremy and started toward the rear of the store.

I've got to trick him, Jeremy told himself. I'll make something up that will scare him into unlocking the door.

"Clem!" Jeremy shouted. "Here come the cops!" He pounded on the door with both fists. "The sheriff's car is on the way!"

The lock clicked. The door opened.

As Jeremy rushed inside the store, Clem took the phone cord out of his pocket and handed it over.

Jeremy plugged the cord into the phone, dialed 911, and quickly reported what had happened and where he was. While he talked, Clem stepped outside, looked both ways, and returned.

When Jeremy hung up, Clem said, "I didn't see any sheriff's car."

"It was probably past before you got out there," Jeremy said.

"You'll say I helped you? You'll tell the cops I let you call?"

"I'll say you let me call. I just hope we didn't waste too much time to save Bonnie."

Jeremy left the store and waited beside the road. Soon he heard sirens in the distance, moving toward him.

A sheriff's car roared into view. Jeremy waved. When the car pulled up beside him, he scrambled into the backseat before it was fully stopped. The sheriff and the game warden who had looked at the bear's carcass were in the car.

As the car sped away from Clem's, Jeremy told the two men everything that had happened.

The sheriff snapped, "We told you kids to stay away from there."

"I'm sorry," Jeremy said.

"Being sorry might not do your pal much good."

"The footbridge to the cabin is just ahead," Jeremy said.

The car stopped.

Jeremy heard more sirens approaching and hoped it was an ambulance.

"You stay in the car," the sheriff said. "No matter what happens, don't get out. That's an order!" He locked the doors.

With their guns drawn, the two men went across the footbridge and disappeared into the woods.

An ambulance pulled up behind the sheriff's car, but nobody got out. Jeremy watched through the rear window. He could tell that the driver was talking on a cell phone or radio.

Don't they know where to go? he wondered. Should I get out and show them?

The driver quit talking but still no one got out.

What are they waiting for? Jeremy thought. Bonnie might need CPR. She might be unconscious.

He started to unlock the door, then remembered what the sheriff had said: "No matter what happens, don't get out." This time he knew he had better do as he was told. Reluctantly, Jeremy stayed where he was.

Maybe the ambulance driver had been talking to the police. Probably the medics had been instructed not to go toward the cabin until they were told it was safe.

Jeremy wanted them to help Bonnie quickly, but he didn't want anyone else to get hurt.

A Highway Patrol car roared up, pulled off the road, and parked in front of the car Jeremy was in. Two officers and a police dog jumped out and ran across the footbridge toward Jeremy's hideout.

Jeremy's imagination kicked into overdrive. Was Bonnie being held hostage? Were these officers from the homicide squad, here to investigate Bonnie's murder?

At least one of the poachers must have escaped, Jeremy thought. The police wouldn't need the dog if the men had been found. The police dog would probably track which way they had gone.

Suddenly the ambulance doors flew open, and three people jumped out. They took a stretcher and other equipment from the back of the ambulance, then hurried down the path.

Jeremy longed to run after them but he stayed

where he was, not daring to disobey the sheriff.

Bonnie must be alive, he thought. The medics wouldn't be in such a hurry if she was dead.

They wouldn't be in a hurry if she was okay, either, he told himself. His throat felt tight, and he blinked back tears.

If Bonnie didn't make it, he would never forgive himself. Never.

CHAPTER
16

Each minute seemed like ten as Jeremy waited.

He imagined what the medics might be doing. He pictured Bonnie, shot in the back and lying unconscious on the path, while the medics knelt beside her. Maybe they had to stabilize her neck before they could move her. Maybe they had to press those electric things to her chest and give her a jolt, as Jeremy had seen on a TV show. Maybe she needed a blood transfusion.

That's what I can do to help, Jeremy thought. I'll donate blood! He tried to open the window, planning to shout to the medics that he would gladly give Bonnie some of his blood, but the electric windows did not work when the engine was off.

Frustrated, he had to wait.

Be realistic, he told himself. Kids are probably not allowed to donate blood, and the medics wouldn't do a transfusion out in the woods. Besides, people had different blood types, and his might not match Bonnie's.

Even so, he planned to offer. It would make him feel a little better if he could help Bonnie in some way, and donating blood might be something he could do.

At last one of the medics emerged from the woods. The other two walked behind him, carrying Bonnie on a stretcher.

Jeremy unlocked the door, leaped out, and ran toward them. Order or no order, he had to find out what had happened, and he knew it must be safe outside the patrol car now. Otherwise the medics would not be bringing Bonnie toward him.

Bonnie's right arm, bent at the elbow, rested on her chest in a splint. She held her left hand over the splint, as if to protect the injured arm from getting bumped. Dirt, streaked with dried tears, smudged her face.

When she saw Jeremy she waved the fingers of her left hand at him.

Jeremy had never been so glad to see anyone,

nor had he ever felt such vast relief. "What happened?" he asked, as he walked near the stretcher. "Did he shoot you?"

"He tried to," Bonnie said. "He shot at me, but he missed." Bonnie talked more slowly than usual, as if she had to search for the words and then push them out.

"I heard the gun go off," Jeremy said. "I was afraid he had killed you."

"He nearly did. I heard the bullet whiz past my right ear." Bonnie closed her eyes.

"I didn't hear a second shot," Jeremy said. "Did he fire again after he missed you, or did you stop running?"

"Neither. The path curved just then, and he couldn't see me for a few seconds, so I ran faster. I thought for sure he would chase me, but he didn't."

"Lucky for you he didn't," said one of the medics. "We'd be carrying you out in a bag if he had."

Jeremy shuddered. "If he didn't shoot you, what happened to your arm?"

Bonnie opened her eyes and blinked at Jeremy, as if trying to remember. Jeremy realized the medics must have given her pain medication that was making her sleepy.

Finally she answered, "I fell and broke my arm.

When I tried to get up, I was dizzy and it hurt so much I was afraid I would faint, so I sat on the path and waited to be rescued. I knew you would go for help as soon as the man started chasing me." Bonnie winced as the stretcher bounced slightly. She looked down at her arm. "I didn't think it would take so long, though. I waited and waited."

"Getting help wasn't easy," Jeremy muttered.

"When the man didn't follow me, I figured he had gone back to get you. I was afraid that you hadn't been able to get away, and I was so scared!" Her words slurred together, as if her tongue were too thick. She closed her eyes again.

The group reached the ambulance.

"We're taking her to the clinic in Lindsburg to get the broken bone set," one of the medics said. "Her mother will meet us there."

"I'll have to tell Mom where I was," Bonnie said. "I'm sorry, Jeremy. I'm really sor . . ." Her voice trailed away.

"I'm the one who's sorry," Jeremy said. "I got you into this mess."

The medic who was not carrying the stretcher opened the back doors of the ambulance.

"What about the poachers?" Jeremy asked as the medics lifted the stretcher into the ambulance. "Did the sheriff and the game warden catch them?"

"Not yet," a medic replied. "They radioed us that Bonnie was on the path, and that it was safe to go that far and bring her out. We haven't talked to them since then."

Bonnie opened her eyes. "Mom went to town to make a bank deposit," she said. "When she didn't answer at home, we tried the cell phone number. It's a good thing she had the phone with her."

I'm glad I didn't take it, Jeremy thought.

One medic climbed in back with Bonnie.

Jeremy wished he could ride along with Bonnie, too, but he knew he had to wait for the sheriff to return.

Jeremy climbed into the backseat of the sheriff's car and watched the ambulance drive away. He had not realized when he walked away from the train wreck that his rash actions would affect so many other people.

He knew he had spent his last night in the hideout. Even if the poachers got caught, he didn't want to stay there by himself any longer.

He would go back to take his money out of the woodpile and get his books, but he would not sleep there tonight. He would call Uncle Ed and go to Chicago. Today, if possible.

A small doubt edged into Jeremy's mind. What if Uncle Ed wasn't home? If he was away on business, his office would know how to contact him, but what if he had taken a vacation? He might be on a remote beach somewhere in the Cayman Islands.

He knew Bonnie would invite him to stay at her house, but he wasn't sure how Bonnie's mom would feel about that. Once she learned that her daughter had nearly been killed, all because Jeremy tried to run away from his troubles, she might never want to see him again, and Jeremy wouldn't blame her.

Grandma would know where to reach Uncle Ed, Jeremy thought. Whenever Mom and Dad had gone somewhere overnight, they had always given Grandma a phone number where they could be reached. Uncle Ed probably did that, too.

The thought of calling Grandma made Jeremy both excited and uneasy. She would be happy to hear his voice and to know that he had survived the train wreck, but she would probably suspect that Jeremy had not really had amnesia all this time. Grandma had a knack for knowing when someone was lying.

I'm going to tell her the truth, Jeremy decided, and admit that I hid in the cabin on purpose. I'll apologize for causing so much heartache and ask everyone to forgive me.

Jeremy pressed his face against the window and watched the path, hoping the police would return soon.

Instead he saw the man who had shot at Bonnie burst out of the woods. The man stopped when he saw the two official cars; then he noticed Jeremy. He ran straight toward Jeremy and yanked open the door.

Too late, Jeremy realized he had not relocked the door after he got out to see Bonnie. I blew it, he thought. I blew it, big time.

"Get out!" the man said.

Jeremy stood beside the car, with his hands in the air.

"Where's your friend?" the man asked.

"I don't know."

"I oughta shoot you right now," the man said. "I should have gone after her, too, instead of letting her run away."

Bang!

Jeremy jumped and looked behind him. The gunshot had come from the east, toward Clem's Country Market.

"Oh, no," the man said. "The cops will find Jeff for sure now." He glanced in all directions, as if unsure what to do next.

"Maybe they already found him," Jeremy said. "Maybe the sheriff fired that shot."

The man pointed the gun at Jeremy.

"If you shoot me," Jeremy said, "the sheriff will hear your gun."

The man looked panicky. "You never saw me," he said. "You got that? You never saw anyone. If you tell the cops otherwise, I'll be back to get you."

Jeremy nodded.

The man ran toward Lake Comstock. As he raced down the road, he took a handkerchief from his back pocket, rubbed it up and down his gun, then tossed the gun in the ditch.

Jeremy waited until the man was far enough beyond the gun that he would not be likely to turn back, then he got in the sheriff's car and honked the horn, over and over.

The man never stopped running. He looked only as big as a toy action figure when Jeremy saw him veer to his right and leave the road.

Jeremy kept honking the horn. The sheriff ran out of the trees toward him.

"The man who shot at Bonnie went that way," Jeremy said. "I can show you where he threw his gun in the ditch. He was almost out of my sight when he ran to the right."

While Jeremy talked, the sheriff got in the car and started the engine. "I'll get the gun later," he said, "after I catch the man."

It took only a minute or two to drive as far as the man had run. "He headed off to the right. Somewhere along in here," Jeremy said.

The sheriff drove slowly. Jeremy scanned the trees, looking for any movement.

Suddenly the sheriff pulled the car onto the shoulder of the road and stopped. "Looks like an old logging road," the sheriff said.

Jeremy could tell that a vehicle had recently driven into the woods at that point.

The sheriff got out just as a brown-and-tan pickup truck bounced toward them on the primitive road.

Jeremy recognized the driver. "That's him!" Jeremy said.

"Get on the floor," the sheriff said, "and stay down."

Jeremy huddled on the floor. He couldn't hear what was said, but he heard the truck door slam so he knew the man must have gotten out. Probably the sheriff was reading the man his rights.

After a few minutes Jeremy's door opened.

"You can ride in front," the sheriff said. Jeremy got out of the car.

The man stood beside the car with his hands cuffed behind his back. His angry scowl made Jeremy turn the other way.

Jeremy got in the front seat; the handcuffed man sat in the backseat. Nobody spoke until the sheriff had started the car and turned it around.

Jeremy asked the sheriff to drop him at the Lindsburg Clinic.

"After I take your statement," the sheriff said.

"He's a kid," the man in back said. "He's too young to testify."

Jeremy did not reply, but he knew he *would* testify. He would tell the sheriff and the game warden everything he knew.

CHAPTER
17

An hour later Jeremy walked into the Lindsburg Clinic. "Is Bonnie Tyland still here?" he asked.

"Yes, but you'll have to wait in the reception area," he was told.

Jeremy sat down. Soon Mrs. Tyland came out of the examining area and sat beside him.

"Hello, Joe," she said. "The doctor is setting Bonnie's broken arm."

"My name isn't Joe; it's Jeremy. It's my fault that Bonnie got hurt." He told Mrs. Tyland everything: how his parents were murdered, how he was on his way to live with his Uncle Ed when the train crashed, how he hid in the cabin, how Bonnie came to see him, how one of the poachers found them, and how he and Bonnie escaped.

He ended by saying, "I'm sorry. I didn't mean to cause trouble for Bonnie. I wanted to run away from my difficulties, to pretend I was on vacation and everything was okay." Jeremy looked down at the floor. "But all I did was make new problems without solving the old ones. I guess I can't hide from reality; I have to face it."

Mrs. Tyland, who had listened quietly to the whole story, said, "The hardest thing in life is to accept the truth."

"I'm going to call my uncle and my grandma and tell them everything," Jeremy said. "Someone will probably come to get me later today. I hope I can see Bonnie before I leave, but if I don't, please tell her thanks for helping me."

"Do you know your grandma's number?" Mrs. Tyland asked.

"Yes."

"Why don't you call her right now?" She removed the cell phone from her purse. After turning it on, she handed it to Jeremy.

As he dialed Grandma's number, he realized his hands were shaking. He heard the ringing sound—once, twice, three times.

"Hello?" Grandma's voice sounded trembly and soft.

"Hi, Grandma. It's me, Jeremy. I'm okay."

"Jeremy?" The quiet voice became a shout: "Jeremy? It's really you?"

It took a while before the conversation could continue, because both sides were crying too hard to be understood.

Arnie sat across from Jeff in the small jail cell, each on a cot.

"Now remember," Arnie whispered. "Stick with our story. We were target-shooting, that's all. We don't know anything about any bears."

"It's probably good I missed the one today," Jeff said.

"Five times." Arnie couldn't help feeling smug, after Jeff had criticized him for missing the last time.

Jeff looked indignant. "Five times?" he said, his voice rising. "What are you talking about? I only shot at him once."

"Shh. Keep your voice down. I heard four shots right after we split up."

"Oh, those," Jeff whispered. "I didn't see a bear then. I was just goofing around, trying to hit some birds."

"You fool," Arnie hissed.

"Just because I missed one bear?" Jeff said.

"I heard those four shots, and I assumed you

had killed the bear. I would never have let that girl get away otherwise. I thought we had time to carry the bear parts to the truck and get out of there, so I went back to the cabin. Even when I discovered that the boy had run off, I didn't worry. I just started calling you, thinking you were nearby, but you didn't answer."

"I never heard you," Jeff said. "I was a ways off by then; it took a while before I saw the bear."

"No surprise, with you scaring him off by shooting at birds."

Jeff spoke louder. "I would have killed the bear with my next shot, only that police dog came running up to me right then."

"Shh. They'll hear you."

"I'm amazed the dog came to me," Jeff continued, "instead of following the bear."

"Will you be quiet?" Arnie said, through clenched teeth. "You can tell me what happened after we get out of here."

The sheriff who had arrested Arnie came over to the cell.

"Bail has been set at five hundred dollars," he said. "Two hundred fifty each."

"We can pay that," Arnie said. He turned to Jeff and said, "Do you have your money with you?"

"What money? I'm broke."

"You had a hundred dollars last night."

"I spent it."

"Spent it!" Arnie said. "How could you have spent it already?"

"I used ten dollars to buy gas and the rest to get my gun out of the pawnshop. That's why I was late this morning; I had to wait for the shop to open."

"You hocked your hunting rifle?"

Jeff shrugged. "I needed cash."

"We need five hundred dollars to post the bond to get out of here. I have four hundred."

Jeff looked surprised. "You've got four hundred bucks? Where'd you get so much cash?"

"I've been saving for a rainy day."

"If I had known you had that kind of money, I would never have pawned my gun. I would have borrowed from you."

"I'll use my four hundred," Arnie said, "but you'll have to come up with rest. Otherwise you'll stay in jail until we go to court. That could take weeks."

Jeff jumped to his feet. His face turned red, and he clenched his fists, as if to take a swing at Arnie. "You'd spring yourself and leave me here?"

"I'm offering to pay part of your bond. If you didn't spend every penny the second it hits your pocket, you'd be able to pay it yourself."

Jeff's eyes narrowed. "You never saved any money before," he said. "You know what I think? I think you kept more than half last night. I'll bet you've kept more than half every time!"

"More than half of what?" asked the sheriff.

"More than half of—"

"Shut up, Jeff!" Arnie said. He stood up and put his hand on Jeff's arm. "I'm your best buddy. Do you think I'd cheat you?"

Jeff stared at Arnie for a moment, then jerked his arm away. "Yes," he muttered. "Yes, I think you would. Why else would you have four hundred dollars in cash today?"

Jeff turned to the sheriff and said, "I did shoot some bears, just like you said."

"Stop it!" Arnie yelled.

Jeff ignored him. "I shot them, and Arnie sold the parts to some guy from Asia. We've been doing it for almost a year now."

Arnie groaned as he sat down and put his head in his hands.

C H A P T E R
18

TO: Jeremy@chic.owt.com
FROM: antiques@lakecom.net
SUBJECT: Hi from Bonnie

Dear Jeremy:
I got your e-mail. I'm glad you made it to
Chicago okay. Mom worried about you flying by
yourself.

My arm doesn't hurt too much. I don't have to
do dishes or write any reports while the cast is on.

I mailed you two newspaper articles. One is
about the poachers getting caught, and the other
is about the train wreck. Your name is in that one.
You're on a list of people who are missing and presumed dead. Weird, huh?

I found out that one of my neighbors, Mr.
Kurten, owns the cabin you used. His grandpa

built it, and Mr. Kurten inherited it when his grandpa died. Mr. Kurten stayed there a few times before he bought his house on Lake Comstock. Nobody uses it anymore, so you probably could have hid out for the whole summer without being discovered. I wish you had, because it is so boring here. I can't even go swimming!

Your friend,
Bonnie

When the newspaper articles arrived from Bonnie, Jeremy skimmed them quickly. He didn't want to read details of the wreck; he only wanted to know if the old man whose initials were JSW had been rescued in time.

The article contained three lists. The first was the names, in alphabetical order, of those who had been killed. Jeremy looked at the end—there was only one last name that began with *W*, and it was a woman's.

Next he read the "missing and presumed dead" list. He found his own name, Jeremy Holland, then continued down to the *W's*. There were two: Marie Whitworth and Robert Wylie.

Daring to hope, he went on to the names of people who had been injured, and that was where he found John Simon Wolff. Mr. Wolff, who had two broken legs, was listed in satisfactory condition.

Dear Mr. Wolff,
I am the boy who talked to you the night of the train wreck. I am glad you survived, and I hope your legs heal fast.

Enclosed is your money clip. I figured out your name from the initials on the clip; then a railroad representative gave me your address after I explained why I needed to write to you. Since the clip is engraved, it should stay in your family.

The money you gave me that night helped me more than you will ever know, even though I didn't need to spend any of it. After I got to Chicago, I donated the money in your honor to the Red Cross, to be used to help victims of future disasters.

Your friend,
Jeremy Holland

To: paul54@tone.net
From: Jeremy@chic.owt.com
Subject: New house

Hi Paul:
Grandma said she called and told you what had happened. When I have more time, I'll give you the details.

Uncle Ed picked me up at the airport and he wasn't mad at me. He told me that grief sometimes makes people say and do things that they would never do otherwise. He said all he cares about is that I'm safe.

It isn't going to be as bad here as I had thought. My room has twin beds, a dresser, a desk, and a big bookshelf. Uncle Ed put a framed picture of Mom and Dad on the desk. I think about them all the time, but it's easier somehow to be in a new place, where memories don't jump out of every corner.

Tomorrow is my first diving lesson at a swim club that Uncle Ed belongs to. I told him I'd rather learn to dive than to play tennis, and that was okay with him.

There is a big library only six blocks away and also a shopping center. Grandma is arranging to have my bike sent here.

Uncle Ed did something really great. He donated a bunch of money to a group that takes in abandoned and abused animals. It was enough for them to build a big new facility. Construction hasn't started yet but when the building is done it will be called the Holland Memorial Shelter, in memory of Mom and Dad.

I miss you and the other guys a lot, but I'm going to make it.

Write soon.
Jeremy

Author's Note

Although the normal life span of a bear is twenty years, the average bear now lives only six years. By then most of them are killed. The U.S. Fish and Wildlife Service estimates that half of the bears who are killed each year are shot by poachers. The rest are shot by licensed hunters during legal hunting seasons.

There are different opinions about whether hunting is ethical. Because animals feel fear and pain, I believe that compassionate people do not kill animals, whether it is legal or not.

If you want to help prevent tragedies such as the killing of Jeremy's parents and bear poaching, here is a pledge that you can copy and sign:

I promise never to use a weapon to settle a dispute.

I promise never to take a gun or other weapon to a public place, such as school, or to show one to my friends.

I will enjoy the outdoors without killing the animals and birds who live there.

Signed: _____

About the Author

PEG KEHRET'S books for young readers are regularly recommended by the American Library Association, the International Reading Association, and the Children's Book Council. She has won "children's choice" awards in seventeen states and has also won the Golden Kite Award from the Society of Children's Book Writers & Illustrators and the PEN Center West Award for Children's Literature. A longtime volunteer at the Humane Society, she often uses animals in her stories.

Peg and her husband, Carl, live in a log house on ten acres of forest near Mount Rainier National Park. Their property is a sanctuary for blacktail deer, elk, rabbits, and many kinds of birds. They have two grown children, four grandchildren, a dog, and a cat. When she is not writing, Peg likes to read, watch baseball, and pump her old player piano.